THE WOODEN BENCH

VERNA FAULRING

ARCHWAY
PUBLISHING

Archway Publishing books may be ordered through booksellers or by contacting:

Archway Publishing
1663 Liberty Drive
Bloomington, IN 47403
www.archwaypublishing.com
1 (888) 242-5904

ISBN: 978-1-4808-7727-6 (sc)
ISBN: 978-1-4808-7726-9 (e)

Library of Congress Control Number: 2019904563

Print information available on the last page.

Archway Publishing rev. date: 05/08/2019

Dedication:

For my beloved Husband, Robert and my children, Patricia, Brian, Roger, Roberta, David and Eileen

1

Joseph Vokil wasn't much at given to cussing. Being a farmer had taught him that no amount of cussing hurried the season or stopped the rain. But a week of steady downpours when it was fruit picking time was beginning to rankle him. The pickers were hired, had to be fed and paid, and all the while sat in the cabins.

There was no one as alert to the ripening season as Joseph Vokil. He roamed the orchards daily, as though without his watchful eye, the trees would not do their part. He knew almost to the day when it was time to stack the baskets outdoors and to hire the pickers. The shipping crates were examined, ready to be examined, ready to be filled with fruit, fruit not quite ready to eat, but firm, just right for shipping. But experience and preparation were meaningless without cooperation from the weather.

The pickers watched from the cabin door as Joseph roamed the orchard, an old hat pulled down on his head, water dripping off the brim, tasting a peach or maybe a pear, eyes search the sky, willing the rain to end.

It was late in the afternoon when the sun finally broke through and Joseph, ignoring the lateness of the afternoon, hustled everyone out to the orchard. The baskets were barely full when the clang of the old dinner bell echoed through the trees.

"Twouldn't hurt none to pick a little longer," Joseph told the workers, but they were already headed in the direction of the house.

"We'll pick after supper till it gets dark," he grumbled to their retreating backs, and glancing at the trees that should have been bare but were still heavy with fruit, he examined the sky. A bright patch of sky promised an evening free of rain. He added a few more peaches to his basket and then he too, walked toward the house.

Seated on a makeshift wooden table with equally rough benches, the workers were quickly engrossed in the business of eating as Charlie, the hired man, filled each plate from the kettle of steaming stew, thick with chunks of beef and home-grown vegetable. Stacks of homemade bread disappeared as slices were speared and dipped in rich gravy.

Two-gallon jugs sat within arms-reach of the men, one filled with water, the other with homemade cider. The water jug remained untouched and Joseph, on his way to the house, stopped, picked it up, and drank thirstily, almost emptying it. Then, glancing at the men, he reminded them, "We'll be pick'n till we can't see our hands in front of us. Get yourselves over there soon as your done eating."

The men nodded and Joseph continued on his way to the house.

"He sure can drink a lot of water. He nearly emptied the jug," one of the men remarked.

"For such a big man like him, it ain't so much," another one said.

Joseph Vokil was indeed a big man, much like his Pa who live on the farm across the way. Not only had he inherited his Pa's stature and girth, he had also inherited his thick black hair and fierce black eyes. Rumor had it that his father, Josuf Vokil, had emigrated from a country constantly over-run by hordes of Turks, Magyars and other fierce invaders, and Josuf was the result of one such invasions.

Whatever his background, everyone knew there had never been a harder working man in the county. The stories of him clearing the land with one horse and his own brute strength were accepted as true and his love of the land was already a legend. His son, Joseph, was almost an exact copy, hard-working, and with a passion for the land that equaled his father's.

Joseph climbed the steps to his house, reminded his two sons eating their supper out on the stoop, that they'd be pick'n again after supper, and went to sit at a place cleared for him at the kitchen table. His wife Alice's acknowledgement of his presence was to put a large plate of food in front of him, the same beef stew as was served to the men outdoors, and like them, he speared a slice of bread, soaked it in gravy, and head bent close to the dish, he forked it into his mouth, wiped the plate clean and handed it to his wife for a refill.

Along with the refill, Alice put two mugs of tea on the table and sat across from her husband. "Have we seen the end of the rain?" she asked him.

Barely glancing up, he told her, "The sun's out and the sky don't look like more rain. We'll pick till dark."

It was all the conversation Alice could expect from a husband who blamed her for having to hire pickers when they might have had sons enough to do the work.

But once he'd been paid for the fruit that was shipped out and the produce that he and Charlie took into the city regularly every week to sell at the open market, and he was satisfied that the vegetable cellar was piled high with plenty to see them till another season, and the shelves were filled with Alice's jellies and pickles, he'd let it be for another year, and accept that she'd not be giving him more sons, and her life would be near pleasant again.

When Karl and Alex had finished eating their supper, Karl handed his brother his dishes. "Take these in the house for me. I gotta go see 'my grandpa.' Tell Pa I'll be back in a while." He said as he hurried in the direction of his grandparent's house.

"'His Grandpa,' that's how it's always been. Never been 'our Grandpa,'" Alex muttered as he stood staring at his brother's retreating back, and felt the resentment building inside him.

"Why am I such a misfit in this land-loving family?" Alex asked himself, the same question he's asked himself a hundred times. "I don't even look like a Vokil. Grandpa, Pa and Karl, they're all alike; big, with black hair and dark eyes."

Grandpa always made fun of my size. "You ain't never gonna be a Vokil with them skinny legs and arms. Where'd ya get them eyes? Nobody in my family ever had blue eyes and hair like yours. It's so pale you kin hardly see you got any."

They were a strange pair, those two, Karl a miniature of his grandpa. He grew up looking just like his grandpa, with Vokil blood in his veins and the same love of the "thick fertile earth."

"I don't think grandpa and me ever liked each other much. We're too different. He knows I don't love the land same as him Karl and Pa."

But for Karl, things are different now. With grandpa ailing, the joy of visiting him will soon be over.

Alex turned away from watching his brother hurrying across the field, took the dishes in the house and went out to get the half-filled basket he'd left out under the tree where he and Karl had been picking.

He had been picking for an hour when Karl returned and joined him in the orchard.

"It'll be dark soon," he told him.

As much as Karl loved this time of year on the farm when the trees were heavy with fruit, and the sweet smell of ripe peaches and pears was like a cloud over the orchard, tonight his mind was on his grandpa and he merely agreed with Alex that it would soon be dark.

The change had been so sudden.

Last summer he had picked fruit with his grandparents and helped crate it for shipping. It wasn't until a late winter snowstorm had buried the entire county that Karl had come face-to-face with the change.

His grandparents had always worked side-by-side, but on that snowy night where he and Alex were shoveling, Karl could only see one head bobbing up and down as he looked across the yard to his Grandpa's.

"I'm goin' to Grandpa's" he hollered to his brother, and as quickly as he could plow his way through the deep snow, he made his way to their house. The bobbing head he'd seen had been his Grandmother's. Karl reached over and took the shovel from her.

"Go in the house, Grandma. I'll shovel."

"Ain't it ever gonna stop snowing?" she asked as she climbed the steps and went into the house.

Karl shoveled to the woodpile and to the barn. When he finished, he filled his arms with a load of wood and took it in the house. Huddled in blankets and hugging the pot-bellied stove was his Grandpa, sound asleep.

Karl stared from one to the other, but before he could open his mouth, his grandmother put her finger to her lip, shushing him.

"It's the medicine from the doctor," she whispered. "It makes him sleepy."

Karl nodded and whispered, "I'll be back later, Grandma."

It did stop snowing and spring did come.

2

It was late when the clop, clop of a horse's hoofs passed the house wakened Karl.

"It's Doc Hallan coming from Grandpa's. I gotta get over and see if my Grandpa's okay," Karl said to himself as he quietly slipped out of bed, hoping not to wake his brother. He groped in the dark for his trousers, pulled them on and tip-toed out of the room.

"Pa's not gonna' like you goin' over there," Alex's voice warned him.

"I didn't mean to wake you," Karl told him, "but I need to know about Grandpa," and ignoring his brother's warning, he ran down the stairs, grabbed his jacket off the hook by the door and was out of the house closing the door behind him.

Even in the dark, Karl had no trouble finding the path that led to his Grandpa's house. The grass had worn away years ago and he could feel the dirt under his bare feet. He hurried across the field, Alex's warning forgotten.

Only a flicker of light showed through the window as Karl climbed the steps. He stood, not sure if he should knock or go in the way he always did, hollerin' so they'd know he was there.

"I better knock," he decided. But before he could lift his hand to knock, his Pa's large frame was blocking the doorway.

"What are you doin' over here?" he demanded gruffly.

Alex was right. His Pa wasn't happy to see him, but he had to know for sure about his Grandpa.

"Did my Grandpa die?" Karl asked, doing his best to keep his voice from shaking.

"Get on home, son," his Pa told him, closing the door, not even letting him in for a quick look at his Grandpa.

"Well, he ain't dead, that's for sure, or Pa would've said so," Karl told himself. He turned and went down the steps, but instead of going home like his Pa told him, he walked around the house to where the old wooden bench sat under the kitchen window and sat down to wait for word about his Grandpa.

Tears suddenly filled his eyes. "We'll never sit out here together again," he muttered sadly. "He'll never be here waiting for me at the end of the day, with a story to tell."

3

Grandpa's decision to come to America and the years he spent working so as to get enough money to buy a 'piece of land all his own' was a story Karl had heard dozens of times, but since he'd started ailin' he seemed only to be remembering his homeland.

Using a tough branch for a cane, he'd stand by the wooden fence, staring out into the distance, "remembering what?" Karl wondered.

Karl pulled his jacket tight around him and with his arms hugging his belly to keep warm, soon he was hearing his Grandpa's voice, telling him the story of the life he'd left behind, a long time ago, before he and Alex were born.

Josuf Vokil, along with his parents and bothers, worked long days in the fields of the rich landowners, earning so little that every night they went to bed with their bellies only half full.

One morning when Johann, who worked next to him in the field, and like him they laughed at the stories they heard about the big land across the sea, failed to appear in the fields, the stories of that big land where man could own a piece of land all his own, began to take hold of Josuf. All day he worked in the field and at night when he went home to share a meager meal with his family, he kept thinking about the stories he'd heard and men who no longer came to work with him in the field, and he began to believe them, that one day he too would go to that land, where he would own a piece of land.

Josuf woke up early one morning while his brothers still slept, nudged his Pa awake, and told him his plans. He too had heard the stories of the land across the sea, so he merely nodded when Josuf told him his plans. He measured out his son's share of the day's food and counted his wages from the pot on the small table next to the statue of Mary, and his Pa with him, they went out to the road, where they stood for a minute gazing at each other, then, with a quick hug, they said goodbye.

With his wages wrapped in a piece of oilskin around his belly, his shoes slung over his shoulder, and carrying a small parcel of food, Josuf set out to find a boat that would take him across the sea where the land he worked would someday belong to him.

Josuf Vokil was a big man, and was used to hard work. He had no trouble working his way in the fields and the vineyards, across the mile that led him to the shipyard, where he put on his boots and was hired to help load and unload the big boats that came from countries around the world.

When he had saved enough money to buy a ticket to America, he boarded a boat and set sail for that land.

It was a journey in a sea so vast it seemed to have no boundaries. When huge waves pounded the boat, he was sure they would all perish, and one after the other, men became sick and died. The boat became an infested tomb where only the hardy survived. By the time they reached America, only a few that had started out, lived to see the land. Josuf was one of those, and when he arrived, he was hired to work on the freighters along the Erie Canal.

For six years, Grandpa worked on the freighters, crossing New York State from Albany to Lockport, loading and unloading tons of goods that contributed to the growth of villages and towns, getting to know the farmers and the merchants along the way, watching the hamlets grow to prosperous towns.

Winters, when the Erie Canal froze and the freighters lay idle,

Josuf rented a room in a rooming house and paid a week's rent, the only time he opened the pouch was to pay for his keep.

Mrs. Johnson, owner of the rooming house, took a shine to the burly young man from Poland and led him to places she knew could use the help during the long winter months.

There were endless jobs of chopping wood for the pot-bellied stoves that were the only source of heat in most homes and shops when the temperatures dropped almost to zero. There were weeks when the snow pile to mountainous heights, and for Josuf, the hours of shoveling were what kept him warm. At night, he slept in his clothes.

Each spring, when the snow and ice melted, and the canal was once again navigable, Josuf was back working the freighters, crossing the state from one end to the other, once again marveling at the growth along the canal, from small hamlets to busy villages.

When talk of the railroad replacing the Erie Canal became more than a rumor, and the crews surveying the land had come and gone, replaced by workers laying ties, and the sound of metal against metal was heard as iron nails were pounded into iron rails, railroads soon replaced the freighters.

Josuf Vogil was unconcerned. His leather pouch, pressing hard against his belly, had enough money to buy a 'piece of land.'

To the north was Lake Ontario where the sunsets were more beautiful than any that Grandpa had ever seen. To the south was Niagara Falls where tourists came to gaze in awe at the mighty cataracts. And not too many miles from either of these, near a small village called Farmington, Grandpa Vokil bought his own piece of land.

Grandpa called his few acres the most fertile piece of land in America.

"Never in my homeland did I see such rich harvests," he'd tell Karl every year as he helped him stow the vegetables in the root cellar.

"We won't have any empty bellies this winter," he'd say and laugh, a hearty satisfied laugh as he patted his belly.

The years passed, but the stories never changed.

For Alex, the stories had long since ceased to interest him, but Karl had continued to cross the field to sit with Grandpa on the bench.

But things were different now. Grandpa was ailing and for Karl the joys of visiting him were almost over.

Karl continued to go over and sit on the wooden bench with his Grandpa, just as he'd done as far back as he could remember. But the joy of storytelling was gone from Grandpa's voice. When he spoke now it was haltingly, gazing off as if trying to remember, "What?" Karl wondered. "Was he back in his homeland? Was he remembering his ma and pa and the rest of his family?"

When he walked he used a stout branch for a cane. The overalls hung loose on his huge frame, and the black eyes had lost their sparkle. The man who used to stand on his back stoop and say, "Look at me!" and boast about his size and brag about his accomplishments was now a shadow of that man. Today, Karl found his visits almost more than he could bear. His Grandpa's life was coming to an end.

The cherries were ripe and ready for picking when Grandpa Vokil died.

There was no consoling Karl. Walking beside him, Alex wanted to reach out, to say something to his brother about their Grandpa dying, but no words came.

"Is it because Grandpa's dying doesn't make any difference to me that I can't say something," he wondered. But after they'd picked for a while he told Karl, "I'm sorry about Grandpa."

Karl acknowledged the words with a quiet grunt and after a while the two boys picked and talked as always, and the sadness side of Karl wasn't as bad as it had been.

It was getting on towards evening when their Pa drove in

from picking Aunt Hulda up at the train station. Aunt Hulda was Grandma's only daughter, who lived in Ohio.

"Where's Uncle Sam and our cousins?" Alex asked his Pa.

"They'll be along," he assured them, and sure enough, just as darkness was beginning to cover the countryside, the wagon drove inside the gate.

Evan as the boys ran to greet their kinfolk, Karl wondered why they had come in a wagon instead of a buggy and why Aunt Hulda had come alone in the train. But Alice and Josif Vokil had walked over to welcome them, inviting them in the house where Alice had a hot dinner prepared, and Karl was left with questions unanswered.

For Alex and his cousins, Peter and Ted, the hours they spent together were like a vacation. They rode the horses down to the lake where they swam in the cold water, screaming and splashing in uninterrupted glee. They went with Alex to visit his friends, the Hawthornes, where they played baseball.

For the Garvey boys and Alex, Grandpa Vokil's death as one of those things that happen to people when they get old and so there was no reason for sadness.

For Karl, the days were painful. He stayed close to his Grandma when his beloved Grandpa was buried, then watched in horror as the men began loading the wagon with Grandma's things. Now Karl knew why they had come in the wagon.

"You're taking Grandma away from her home when the feel of Grandpa's still here," Karl accused his Aunt Hulda.

"Karl, she's my Ma. I can't leave her here alone," Hulda explained. "Besides, she's getting old too and needs someone to take care of her." Karl walked away from her and went to sit on the bench to watch as the house was emptied and crates and furniture were tied down on the wagon. When there was nothing left but the bare walls, the Garvey's went over to share a hot dinner with the Vokil's before leaving for home.

Karl sat a while lingering, staring at the empty house and the wagon loaded with all his Grandparent's possessions, and it seemed to him that a whirlwind had rushed in, and when it moved on, there was nothing left of the life he'd known.

"You'll come visit me, won't you?" their Grandma asked the boys, then kissed them both, as the Garvey's were ready to leave.

"Soon as spring planting's over," Karl promised. Their Grandma kissed them both and Joseph helped his mother into the buggy for the ride to the train station.

Later, Karl complained to his Pa about Aunt Hulda and her family coming and taking their Grandma away.

"We could've taken care of her," he said.

"If I thought she'd be unhappy, I'd have argued with Hulda, but she won't be so lonely with them," Joseph told his son. "Your Grandma always like your Uncle Sam, and enjoyed talkin' with him. And him bein' a Reverend, she'll get to go to church regular and get to know the neighbors. Church people are friendly people," Karl. "Your Grandma'll be fine."

Karl knew his Pa was right, but it didn't take away the emptiness inside him.

Almost overnight, the house across the field had lost all signs of life. Joseph Vokil moved the animals to his barn and told the boys, "Tomorrow after school you two boys can load the wagon with the hay that's in the loft and get it over to our barn."

"When are we supposed to get our homework done?" Alex grumbled. But the next afternoon the boys were loading the hay on the wagon.

"When we get the hay loaded, will you help me put the bench on the wagon?" Karl asked his brother.

"What you want with that old wooden bench?" Alex asked.

"I just want you to help me get it home," Karl snapped, tossing the hay down with such venom. Alex was surprised it landed on the wagon. He turned away from his brother, determined to ignore his quick spurt of anger, waiting for him to be his old self again.

Back home, Alex helped Karl get the bench off the wagon and they set about the tiring chore of unloading the hay.

When they had finally pitched the last forkful into the barn, the boys dropped down onto the hay, exhausted.

"Seems like all we do is work," Alex complained. "Once school starts we shouldn't have to do all this extra. We don't have time to do our homework."

"Getting the hay over was all that was left to do," Karl told him. "There's nothing but empty buildings over there now," and getting up he told Alex, "I better move the bench."

"Where you gonna put it?" Alex asked.

"Under the kitchen window, where else?" Karl said.

"That bench isn't comfortable no matter where you put it," Alex told him. "We oughta' build us a new one, one that's not warped from sitting out all these years."

"We're not building us a new bench," Karl shouted angrily.

Though it shouldn't have, the anger in Karl's voice surprised Alex and when Karl brushed the hay off the bench and sat down, Alex chose to sit alone under the oak tree.

"Karl knows that bench doesn't have good memories for me, but he doesn't need to worry. I'm not gonna take the axe to it," Alex muttered to himself and after a few minutes he decided to go in the house.

"I'm goin' in the house and get some homework done," he told Karl.

Sitting out on the bench alone, Karl regretted the way he'd talked to his brother when Alex had mentioned building a new bench. I can't expect this old bench to mean anything to him, and talking mean won't change the way he feels about Grandpa or the farm.

"We're sure different, Alex and me," Alex reflected as he sat staring at the spot where Alex had sat.

"I'm a Vokil, big, with the same black eyes and hair as Grandpa and Pa." Karl smiled at the way his Grandpa used to boast he was a descendant of the Turks and Magyars and that's where they got their looks.

"But Alex, there've been times when I've envied his blue eyes and light hair. There's a kindness, a gentleness about him the Vokil's don't have. Grandpa called it the soft face, not a lot of character. But it was more than the color of Alex's hair or his blue eyes that bothered Grandpa. It was a meanness because Alex was indifferent to him and didn't love the land."

But Alex not liking the land frightened Karl. "What's to become of someone who hates the farm the way Alex does?" Karl asked himself. Worrying about Alex won't change anything, so Karl decided to go into the house.

Alex sat at the kitchen table, his books spread in front of him, concentrating on his homework. Over by the window, his mother sat in her rocking chair reading. Karl got his books and went over to sit next to his brother at the table, but his earlier nastiness towards Alex nagged at him until finally he told Alex, "I'm sorry for the way I talked to you outside."

Alex looked up from his notebook and turned to face his brother, "I'm tired of the way you've been talking to me since Grandpa died. It's as if you're mad because you know I'm not grieving. Well, do I have a reason to grieve, Karl? Do I?" Alex asked angrily, and before Karl could say a word, Alex had closed his books and was on his way upstairs.

Surprised at the outburst, so unlike Alex, Karl knew there'd be no homework done today and closed his books.

"Maybe Alex's spouting off a little will make some of the hate go away," Alice said.

"It'll take more than a little spouting off," Karl told his Ma as he picked up his books and went upstairs. Alex was stretched out on his bed reading.

"What are you reading?" Karl asked casually, hoping his wasn't still angry.

"It's one of those books Grandma gave me when they were emptying the house. There's a few under the bed anytime you feel like reading," Alex said and he didn't sound mad.

"I didn't know Grandma liked to read. I know I never saw Grandpa with a book," Karl said.

"That's because Grandpa didn't know how to read," Alex said with undisguised scorn.

"How do you know that?" Karl asked, angry with his brother's tone of voice.

"Grandma told me she taught him to write his name, but he never learned to read. Grandpa was never interested in anything but land, land, land."

The minute the words were out of his mouth, Alex regretted them, and told Karl.

"Every time we mention Grandpa it seems like we're looking for a fight. How I feel about Grandpa's not important. What is important is what it's doing to you and me. If we keep on this way, we'll end up hating each other."

Alex's voice shook with emotion, and Karl, quick to accept the blame told him. "It's my fault. I can't get used to Grandpa being dead and Grandma gone to Ohio and the house across the field empty."

"It's not important whose fault it is. Let's just cut out this needling each other every time Grandpa's mentioned," Alex said, and then told Karl, "You need to get away from the farm for a few hours."

"It'll be good for Karl to get away from the farm for a few hours," Alice told Alex when he came with a sack for her to fill with food. "Maybe he'll learn that it's time he made friends."

Alex merely nodded as his mother filled the sack with potatoes they'd bake in the fire and sausage and fresh bread and gingersnaps.

"Come Saturday after we get the barn cleaned out, a bunch of us guys are getting together at the Hawthornes. We're gonna' have one of our wild ball games then ride down to the lake for a swim and later build a fire in the sand and have a cookout. Wanna' come?" he invited him.

"Yea, I sure would," Karl said with an enthusiasm that surprised himself as well as Alex.

"Have a good time," Alice told Alex and stood at the window watching her sons as they raced out the gate and onto the road, wondering as she did so often now that Alex was getting older, what the future held for him. "He'll never stay on the farm. Karl will, but not Alex," she told herself and turned away from the window.

Spring, summer, fall, winter and planting and harvesting, the cycle never changed. The boys worked side-by-side with their Pa and Charlie, the one loving the farm, the other hating it.

Driving home from town one afternoon where they'd gone to pick up a bag of flour for their Ma, Alex told his brother, "I'll be eighteen in a few weeks. I'm leaving the farm."

"Where will you go, Alex? What will you do?" Karl asked anxiously.

"Get a job somewhere. Do something besides pick fruit and do stinking farm chores," he answered with his usual distaste for the farm. Then, watching his brother's face for his reaction, Alex told him, "I plan on going back to school and then to college."

Stunned, Karl tried to remember if he knew anyone who went to college.

"There's no one we know went to college except Doc Hallen. Why do you want to go?" Karl asked him.

"I want to be a doctor," Alex said, sitting up straighter, pleased with his announcement and Karl's reaction when he said, "A doctor, Alex!"

Surprise was turning to awe and admiration. "Pa'll sure be happy!" Karl told him.

Alex banged the reins on the horse's backs, "Come on, you lazy animals, get a move on." Then he told his brother, "I don't think Pa'll be happy. Not one bit happy. He wanted me to quit school, didn't he?" Alex said angrily.

"But he let you keep going for another year," Karl reminded him. "And there's so much extra work with Grandpa's farm added to ours."

"Pa oughta sell Grandpa's farm" Alex said.

"Sell the land! Sell Grandpa's land!" Karl said staring at his brother, horrified.

Unmoved by Karl's reaction, Alex told him, "Then Pa oughta get another hired man instead of piling the extra work on his sons."

"I'll soon be sixteen and not going to school no more. I'll be home all day to help,"

Karl told his brother, but he knew that wouldn't stop Alex from leaving the farm. But wanting to go to college, well, that was different.

But as the days passed, Alex seemed strangely quiet, not mentioning his plans, not even grumbling about the work and the smell of the farm. It's just not natural for him to clean the barn without grumbling. "What's he thinking about these days?" Karl wondered, and before too long he knew.

4

In the spring of 1917, Alex Wokil was eighteen years old and the United States joined forces with Europe to defeat Germany. A conscription law was passed in May, but Alex had already joined the army, had completed his training and was home on a short leave, before being shipped overseas.

Karl remembered the exact day his brother had decided to join the army.

The early rains had kept the grounds too wet for planting, so their Pa decided to take a trip into Farmington, "to see what the folks are saying about the President wantin' to send our boys over to end that war goin' on in Europe."

"You feel like ridin' in, Alice?" he asked his wife. Then turning to the boys, he told them, "You two can come along if your chores are done."

"Guess a lot of farmers had the same idea as me," Joseph remarked when he saw the buggy's lined up along Main Street.

"You boys can let your Ma and me off and find a spot for the buggy," he told them.

The boys waited for their Ma and Pa to get down from the buggy, then sat watching them as they headed toward their favorite meeting places. Pa was on his way to Wieppes Hardware store, the biggest store on Main Street, where you could usually find a group of men exchanging the latest news and discussing the running of the country.

Across the street was Deke's Bar where the men ended up when Dan Wieppes, tired of the loud voices and their cigar smoke that smelled up his store, pushed them out.

"Ma's on her way to Moores," Karl told Alex, grinning as he watched her move with a spry step in the direction of the shop where Mrs. Moore sold yarn goods and ribbons and buttons and other 'frou-frous' for women and their daughter, and where you could hear the latest gossip.

When they'd found a place to park the buggy, Alex suggested, "Let's wander down to Scheiner's lot. That's probably where the guys are."

The empty lot next to the grocery store was already alive with local as well as farm boys. Alex went over to join a group of his friends and Karl, hearing their excited voices followed.

"What do you think Alex?" Steve Hawthorne asked his friend as Alex walked toward the group.

"I'm still thinking," Alex told him.

"My Pa says that if the President gets us in the war we won't have no choice about going," Dale Wieppes said.

"You thinking of joining up," Steve asked him.

"Yea, I'm thinking I might," Dale answered, sounding like he'd already made up his mind.

The voices grew louder as questions were asked and decisions were weighed. As the group grew larger, the eagerness and excited voices were too much for Karl. Heart pounding with fear at the thought of his brother going off to war, Karl left the group and wondered back down Main Street where he sat on the bench outside Demler's Repair shop.

"Pa'll surely not let Alex go off to war when he's got his heart set on being a doctor," Karl reasoned. But the eagerness of the voices in Schiener's lot rang in his ears.

Back in the hardware store, Doug Wieppes was urging the men outside.

"You're smelling the place up awful," he told them as heavy odor of pipe tobacco filled the store.

"All the arguin' in the world ain't gonna change the President's mind once he's decided what he's gonna do."

In Mrs. Moore's shop, the women pretended not to be interested in any of the latest stories going around, but the craned necks belied their words.

5

In June of 1917, the United States entered the war, but Alex Vokil and some of his buddies hadn't waited for the formal declaration. Along with Steve Hawthorne and Dale Wieppes, Alex had taken the train to Buffalo, found a recruiting station and joined the army. Now, a few weeks later, Alex was home, handsome in his khaki uniform, buttons shined bright, boots spit polished, puttees wound tight almost to his knees.

For the Vokil's, Joseph and Alice, there was shock and disbelief at the sight of their son in uniform. For Karl, there was regret and sadness.

"I haven't felt so much sadness since Grandpa died," Karl told Charlie, the hired man, when the two of them were working out in the orchard.

Everybody says the war'll be over fast now that America's in it. "Alex'll be home in no time," Charlie told Karl, then added, "Maybe the farm will look good to him when he gets back."

Karl went on working, not saying nothing. He knew better.

The night before Alex was to leave, the boys went out to sit on Grandpa's bench for a final visit.

It was a pleasant evening, a slight breeze rustling the leaves of the oak tree, and a bright red sunset promised another good day for working in the orchard. But neither Alex nor Karl had their minds on the orchard.

"You told me your plans a while ago, Alex. What made you change your mind and join the army?"

"All I did was jump the gun a couple of months. I wouldn't have no choice now any way,"

Alex told Karl. "Besides, it'll feel good getting away from the farm."

"But joining the army, Alex, that strikes me as being a little extreme. What about your plans for school and college?"

"They're still my plans, Karl. Everybody says now that the United States is in the war, it'll be over in no time."

"You shoulda' talked to Pa..."

"Karl," Alex interrupted, "I still would have to go in the army, no matter what plans I had. But I did talk to Pa."

"You did?" Karl looked at his brother, hardly able to ask the next question. "What did he say?"

There was no mistaking the resentment in Alex's voice when he answered. "If he'd agreed to send me to school, would I have been in such a hurry to join the army?"

Karl shook his head, not in disbelief, but in disappointment.

"Grandpa told us about the rich landlords in his hometown and Pa's no different," Alex said bitterly. "He bought Grandpa's land and he's got his mind on that empty lot at the end of our property. He figures on someday planting a vineyard."

"How do you know all this?" Karl asked.

"Pa told me that buying Grandpa's land left him strapped and Charlie told me about the vineyard. So where would the money come from to send me to college?" Alex asked angrily. "Land, land, land, always the land. That's all the Vokil's can think about."

"It's so different how we see things," Karl told his brother. "Grandpa always said there's nothin' like the land, and that's how I feel too. I've always been content on the farm, never once wanted to leave it."

"Your thinking has always been influenced by Grandpa," Alex told him, not unkindly.

Karl looked at his brother, shaking his head sadly.

"I miss him, Alex. No matter that you and him never got along. I loved him."

"Yea, I know," Alex said. "Remember that awful fight we had when I was teasing you about Grandpa and his stories. You were mad cause I called them tall tales."

"I remember," Karl said. "I thought we'd kill each other. We went after each other like a couple of animals."

"When Grandpa died, I wanted to tell you how sorry I was, and that I'd only been teasing about the tall tales, but I didn't think you'd believe me." Alex hesitated, then in a quiet voice, continued, "We were never friends, Grandpa and me. I could never understand why the color of my hair or my blue eyes bothered him. I quit going over, not because I got tired of listening to his stories, but because he always made me feel like it didn't matter to him if I was there or not."

"You know, Karl, in the army, they don't care about the color of your hair or the color of your eyes. And it doesn't matter to them if your legs are fat or skinny. All that matters, is that you can hold a rifle and learn to shoot."

The bitterness in his brother's voice was too much for Karl to bear. He got up and walked over to the big oak tree in the middle of the yard and stood under it. The thought of Alex's unhappiness frightened him. He's gone and joined the army to get away, to maybe rid himself of all the hate that's been eating away at his insides.

"I never knew how bad it was, I never knew!" Karl felt the tears sting his eyes but the daylight had gone so Alex probably wouldn't notice.

Alex came to stand with him. Even with the daylight gone, he could see the glassy look in his brother's eyes and wished he hadn't spoken so harshly.

"I didn't mean to upset you, little brother," Alex told him. "You and me, it's always been alright between us. Unless I reminded you, I don't think you noticed how different we were." Then to change the subject, Alex asked, "Do you have any plans, or are you just waiting to grow up a little more?"

Karl reached to give his brother a punch but Alex saw it coming and moved out of harm's way.

The joshing lifted the sadness that had begun to envelop them, and Karl told Alex, "When Grandma went with Aunt Hulda to Ohio, I saw the farm belonging to me one day. I had Sally in mind. On my seventeenth birthday I was thinking of talking seriously to her, asking if I could court her. I was going to ask Pa if over the winter I could do a few more repairs on the house so Sally and me could marry when I turned eighteen." Alex told him.

"Pa'll probably be delighted for you to marry and live there. He sure wouldn't want the house left empty much longer," Alex told him.

"Will he sell it to me, or will I have to be a tenant farmer?" Karl bristled, suddenly unsure of his Pa's plans.

"Don't get your dander up. Wait till Pa gets over my leaving," Alex advised him. "He'll be glad to have you stay on the farm and he'll probably give you the house."

"Ya sure?" Karl's tone was flat.

Alex moved away from the tree toward the house. "Time for me to go in, Karl. Hawthorne's will be here early to pick me up and I want to sit with Ma for a while."

Karl followed his brother into the house. A small shaft of light picked up their Ma sitting in her rocker. Alex went over to sit next to her. Karl said good night and went up to bed. Alice Vokil reached for her son's hand, still cold from the outdoors.

"I always knew you'd leave the farm someday," she told him,

"but going off to war, Alex." Alice shook her head. She had no words to express her feelings. Alex leaned over and put his arm across her shoulder.

"Ma, I'll be home before you know it," he told her, hoping to reassure her, "and when I do come home, I'm going back to school and live somewhere where I'll never have to smell manure again."

"Most farmers don't even notice the smell of manure," his mother lied, remembering how her brothers fought about whose turn it was to clean the barn.

"You know it's more than the smells, Ma" Alex told her. "You understand I'm just not cut out for farming, don't you?"

"Yes, I understand that, but you're going off to war. I'll miss you," she said sadly. Alex knew his mother was crying and felt tears rolling down his own cheeks.

"I'll miss you too, Ma." He told her.

They sat a while longer, Alice rocking, neither saying anything more until his Ma told him, "Morning will be here before we know it. We'd better get some rest."

The goodbyes between Alex and his Ma and Pa were emotionally restrained. Only Karl's unwillingness to let go of Alex's hand brought a look of wistfulness to his brother's eyes.

"I'll miss you," Alex told him.

"I'll miss you too," Karl said.

They parted.

The wagon was already moving out of the yard when Joseph Vokil ran outside and hollered, "I'll ride in with you Steve."

6

Alex had left during the lull between planting and harvesting and for Karl, the summer had been long, hot and lonely. "I don't remember picking fruit being such tedious work," Karl told himself one particularly hot day. "If Alex was here, we'd go dunk our heads in the water barrel to cool off, or maybe after supper for a ride over to Hawthorne's to swim in their pond."

"I hope the war ends soon," Karl told his father as they walked together out of the orchard.

"Life's different with Alex gone."

"Talk is it won't be long till our boys'll be comin' home."

Though Joseph Vokil had been upset at Alex having to go off to fight a war in a strange country. It never occurred to him that Alex wouldn't survive the war and return home. But Alex Vokil was one of the boys that wasn't coming home.

When the news came that Alex had been killed in action, there was no display of anger, no ranting and raving against the injustice and futility of war. Joseph read the letter, and in stunned silence handed it to his wife. When she cried out in anguish, her husband put his hand on her shoulder, held it there for a minute, then left the house. Karl held his mother, his arm tight around her. After a bit she released herself and went upstairs. Karl went out to sit on the bench he and Alex had shared not so long ago, staring off into nowhere, unable to grasp the reality of his brother's death.

He hadn't heard his mother come out, but she was there beside him. Her hand reached out for his. Karl held it tight in his own.

"Did you know he wanted to be a doctor?" he asked her.

"No, I didn't know," she said sadly. "I only knew he was unhappy on the farm and planned to leave."

"Even if there was no war, he'd have left," Karl told her. "He hated digging in the dirt and shoveling manure, and I hated his complaining. He couldn't wait to get away from the farm,"

"You're like your Pa and Grandpa about the land, you'd never have understood."

It was an accusation Karl was quick to set straight.

"But I did understand, Ma," he told her with a burst of anger. "When he explained how important it was for him to finish school and go to college and someday be a doctor, all I felt was relief that he'd found something to take the place of the farm."

His Ma started to cry again and Karl, knowing there were no words he could say to console her, sat quietly by her side, her hand in his, until after a while she got up to go into the house.

7

The war ended. The Armistice was signed. The event was not mentioned in the Vokil household, as life on the farm seemed to go on as before. But Karl felt a change in their lives. Busy as they were, working from early morning until sundown, sometimes later when the fruit had to be crated and taken to town. The bees buzzing in the orchard made more noise than they did. Pa, when he brought baskets of fruit into Ma to put down, didn't brag about the rich harvest like he used to.

"He's quiet alright, grieven'," Charlie said when Karl asked about his Pa.

"Your Pa ain't much for a lot of words, but losin' a son… it takes a lot of gettin' over," Charlie told him.

Karl, wrestling with his own grief and loneliness, merely nodded agreement.

Winter was long and cold. Outdoors, fierce winds blew the snow into mountainous drifts so that the narrow paths to the barn and the woodpile were hemmed in by walls of snow.

Indoors, the Vokil family, unable to lift themselves out of the depression that settled in after Alex's death, was enveloped in a wall of silence. During the evenings around the potbellied stove, Pa read his bible and Ma sat knitting. The only break in the silence was a log crackling or the click of mom's knitting needles. With the snow closing them in, the world beyond the farm seemed remote and unreal.

"Is it grief or remorse that's plaguing Pa?" Karl asked his Ma one night after his father had gone to bed.

"There's no talking between your Pa and me about Alex, so I don't rightly know," she told him. Then to cover the harshness of her words, she said, "T'won't be long till spring. We need a bit of sunshine. Once your Pa has spring planting to keep him busy, he'll ease up."

As winter loosened its grip and the sun began to shine, the piles of snow began to melt until one day Karl could see clear across the field to his Grandpa's empty house. Seeing it he felt a sadness, so much a part of him now that the two people he loved dearly were gone.

8

Spring did come.

The trees were in bud, the birds had returned to chirp and warble and build their nests. In no time at all, the apple orchard would be a mass of color and sweet-smelling blossoms, and Karl working side-by-side with his Pa and Charlie, realized his Ma had been right. Spring had lifted not only Pa's spirits, but all their spirits. But for him, the reminders of Alex's absence was there, and loneliness was the hardest for him to deal with.

"Now that the weather's warmer and traveling's easier I need to get over to Rief's and talk to Sally," Karl decided. "I shoulda' done it a long time ago."

Karl still hadn't discussed the empty house with his Pa. The months had flown by and he hadn't felt like approaching him, waiting for a sign that he was his old self again. Now that his eighteenth birthday wasn't far off, he decided it was time to start giving serious thought to his life.

Sunday morning Karl rushed through his chores, hurrying to get cleaned up and rushing out the door he told his Ma, "I'm going to church in Farmington."

"Must be he's got Sally Rief on his mind.," she decided and watched as he drove off in the buggy.

In church, Karl was barely aware of the services. His eyes and thoughts were on Sally. He smiled broadly when she looked his way. Her smile in return was half-hearted, not at all encouraging.

But what could he expect? He hadn't called on her for weeks and weeks, months actually. She'll understand, he assured himself.

Outside, after service, Karl hurried to her side.

"How are you, Sally?" he asked, feeling awkward now that they were face-to face. He had forgotten how pretty she was. Her dark hair hung almost to her waist, a silver clip holding it in place, accentuating her oval face. The eyes that looked back at him were as blue as he remembered, but not welcoming. "Hello Karl," she said without warmth.

Karl had come prepared to make up for his long absence and so, ignoring her coolness, he asked her, "I wondered if I could drive you home."

"You ready, Sally?" Pete Korsa was suddenly beside her. Seeing Karl, he went over to shake his hand.

"We wondered if you'd left the area," Pete told him. "Nice to see you," and taking Sally's hand, he led her to the buggy.

Karl drove home slowly. The good feeling, the hopes he'd indulged in during his ride to the church, how quickly they'd been shattered.

"You can't expect a pretty girl like Sally to sit around waiting for you," his mother told him when she heard his sad tale. "You shoulda' been goin' to church regular, you might have had a chance then."

Disappointed as he was, Karl had no time to mope. There was planting to be done, two big gardens, their own as well as the one on Grandpa's land. It seemed the planting was no more than over when the ripening began. Pa was already out in the orchard checking the fruit. The early cherries and the first picking of greenings were about ready to pick.

9

Soon the ripening and harvesting began to run together and the enthusiasm was back in Pa's voice when he came in the house, loaded down with a big basket of freshly picked vegetables and fruit.

"Look at these," he'd say to Ma. "Have you ever seen anythin' like 'em? We'll have a fine load to take to the market tomorrow."

Listening to his father, Karl remembered how Alex used to react to such jubilation over the rich harvest.

"That rich, black earth that produces such a bountiful harvest. Isn't that what it's supposed to do?" he'd say.

The first touch of fall was in the air when Karl and Charlie were doing the final stripping of the apple trees. They'd picked from dawn to dusk each day until the fruit trees were almost bare and now as they carried the last basket of apples to the shed, Charlie told Karl, "I can't believe we're done for another year. Once we get these apples crated and to the cannery we can sit and do a bit o' nothin' now and then."

Karl smiled at the thought of Charlie doing a bit o' nothin'. Sometimes him and Pa'd sit on the ground under the oak tree and drink a pitcher of cold water. "I guess that's what Charlie means about doin' a bit o' nothin'."

"You and Charlie can load the crates on the wagon after supper," Joseph told his son. "We'll get an early start to the cannery."

"Who's we?" Karl asked.

"You an me," his father told him.

Karl had hope Charlie would go with his Pa. The trip to the Markville cannery was long and wearisome, and he and his Pa never had much to say to each other.

It was barely daybreak when they climbed onto the wagon and headed out. Once past the trees, out in the open, Joseph examined the sky.

"Not much of a day," he told his son. "No sign of the sun coming up."

"Kinda' early to tell." Karl said."

"Don't look promising with all them clouds," his father replied.

They drove in silence until Joseph started talking about the harvest. Karl, tired of the same talk as every night at dinner, let his thoughts drift.

"Except for the potatoes and pumpkins, we're about finished for the year. And there's lots of time before we need to get them in. It'll give us time to pull down the old house."

Hearing his father's words, Karl's body stiffened. "Pull down the house?" he asked, though he knew exactly what his Pa was talking about.

"My Pa's house," his father told him. "You know of any other house needs tearing down?"

Karl jumped off the wagon. "You tear Grandpa's house down and I'm leaving and never coming back," he shouted angrily.

"Whoa there, "Joseph pulled the reins to slow the horses and called to Karl, "Now son, you and me got some talkin' to do. You just climb back up here and listen."

The clouds, grey when they started out, had turned black without father or son noticing, until without warning, a thunderbolt crashed around them. The horses reared up and Karl watched in horror as his father was yanked off the wagon seat to fall under the hoofs of the frightened horses.

Karl rushed to quiet the horses, unhitched them, then carefully lifted his father's battered body onto the wagon. By now the rain, whipped by a sudden wind, was thrashing against them. Karl tore off his shirt to cover his father, rehitched the horses to the wagon and turned in the direction of his house.

Charlie came running toward the gate when he saw the wagon. His cry of pain at the sight of Joseph became a long, agonized moan as he jumped on the wagon and led the horses to the house. Together they carried Joseph inside. Karl tried to shield his mother but she pulled aside the wet shirt and when she saw her husband's mutilated face, she collapsed without so much as a whimper. "Stay with Ma," Karl told Charlie. "I'm going for Doc Hallan."

10

Doc Hallan brought Mrs. Turner out to stay with Alice and gave Karl orders to keep a close watch on his mother.

"It'll be a while before she gets over the shock of what happened, of being alone without a husband," Doc Hallan told Karl. She needs comforting. Maybe a visit with her family would be good for her.

Karl agreed and when his mother was up to it, he asked Charlie to drive her to her folks in Bolton.

Karl was glad his mother was being cared for, but for him, the organized, predictable life he had known was chaos as he struggled with the problems of running the farm without his Pa. Charlie was there, but since Pa's death, it seemed his mother needed him. There'd been the two-day trip to take his mother to Bolton to see her folks, and soon there's be the trip to pick her up. Working alone, Karl brooded over his father's death, guilt hanging over him like the dark cloud that caused it. If he hadn't been so rash, hadn't jumped off the wagon, they would have noticed the dark clouds and Pa would have had a tight hold on the reins.

When Charlie came back from Bolton with his mother, Karl was relieved that now he'd be able to count on Charlie's help. But now that she was home, it seemed that his mother was using Charlie every couple of days to drive her to Farmington.

Coming into supper one evening, bone tired as always, Karl filled his plate from the kettle on the stove, cut several slices of bread and sat down across from his mother. "Ma, we're going to have to hire another man," he told her. "There's more work than one man can handle."

"I've been using Charlie to help me. It's not fair to you, I know," she apologized.

"Marty Gluck's not doing much of anything these days, or at least he wasn't the last time I saw him. I could talk to him," Karl suggested.

Alice sat sipping her tea, intently examining her son. Karl sensed her hesitation. "You got something against Marty?" he asked her.

"Finish your dinner, son, then maybe we can sit outside and talk," she told him.

"What's on her mind?" Karl wondered and suddenly the trips back and forth to town took on an ominous foreboding. Gulping down his supper, he poured his tea and told his mother, "let's go talk."

She followed him out. "It's pleasant sitting out this time of day. The sun has moved to the front of the house and there's most always a breeze," she said as they settle on the bench. And then without a hint of warning, she told her son, "I've sold the farm."

Karl's immediate reaction was that his mother was mad. "Are you out of your mind? Has Pa's dying made you take leave of your senses? Sell the farm?" Karl realized he was shouting.

When his mother simply sat watching him and made no attempt to answer him, did not argue with him, his disbelief turned to fury.

"You had no right! You had no right!" he shouted, and jumping to his feet and standing menacingly in front of her, he continued his tirade.

"It's not yours to sell. This is my home, yours and mine and you have no right to sell it."

When Alice saw there was no end to his raving, she raised her hand to silence him and told him, "You cannot run the farm alone."

"Charlie's here and I can hire help," Karl told her.

"Karl, Karl," she pleaded, "Will you listen to me... the heart has gone out of me. We need to get away from the farm."

"Maybe you need to get away from the farm, but the farm is mine, mine, mine. Grandpa and Pa..."

She cut him off. "The farm is sold." The finality in her voice, the abruptness of her words silenced him. He stood staring at her. She moved toward him, but Karl ran to the barn, saddled his horse and climbed up on it. Standing in the doorway was Charlie. "Listen to me, Karl," he begged.

"Get out of my way or I'll run you down," Karl threatened. Charlie moved.

Karl rode across the farm and out onto the road in the direction of Farmington, but suddenly he didn't want to go into town to be with people. He rode a short distance and turned toward a large clump of trees, the dividing line between the Vokil farm and a vacant piece of land. He lowered himself from the horse, tied it to a branch and began to pace, back and forth, back and forth, between the trees. "You have no right," he kept shouting as he pounded his fist against the tree trunk, then kicked the ground until the dust was flying all around him. He dropped to the ground, and leaning against a tree he talked to his Grandpa.

"If you'd have been here, none of this would have happened. You'd never let anyone sell the farm. There's nothing as important as the land! We know that, don't we Grandpa?"

Karl continued to rile against his mother, to holler against her and her foolishness until finally, overcome with exhaustion, he buried his head in his arms and recognized the feeling of defeat as misfortune piled up. And yet... "to give up the farm, Ma must be a little out of her head. Too many things have gone wrong. Losing

Alex, and now Pa. She's left with too much responsibility. Pa always took care of things."

Karl began to realize he'd given no thought to his Ma.

How come I never thought how hard this must have been for her? How come I never realized her heart must be broken? First losing a son and now Pa. How could I have been so thoughtless? But even as he tried to see the sadness in his mother's life, he could not believe she would do anything so crazy as to sell the farm.

Exhausted, Karl climbed back on the horse and headed for home. He stabled the horse and went to sit alone on the wooden bench, too weary to climb the steps into the house.

Charlie came and stood in front of him. "You all screamed out?" he asked sarcastically. Karl ignored the nasty remark, not even looking up.

"I've been wanting to tell you about your Ma, the reason she wants to get away from the farm," he said.

Karl was not interested in anything Charlie had to say, especially if it concerned the farm. He realized resentment had been building for weeks. Him left with all the chores and Charlie off to Farmington with Ma. Ma knew how to drive a buggy. Charlie knew all about selling the farm when his mother hadn't even mentioned it to her own son.

"What else does Charlie know?" Karl wondered.

"Your Ma's pregnant."

Squinting off in the direction of an almost dark sky, Karl seemed not to have heard.

"You're Ma's pregnant," Charlie repeated. "Doc Hallan says if she miscarries again, she could die."

Charlie's words hit Karl with the impact of a bullet and his anger blazing, he lashed out at him. "Get the hell off this farm before I kill you," Karl shouted savagely.

His mother, standing on the steps, could barely contain her rage. "The child I carry is your Pa's," she cried out.

"Pa's dead," Karl reminded her.

"That's so," she shot back. "And this child is his!" She turned and went back in the house. Charlie headed for the barn.

Karl sat alone on the bench, horrified at the accusation and stunned by this new bombshell. He pulled his jacket tight around him to ward off the cool night air as well as the feeling of desolation that was gnawing at him. Grandpa's dying, then Alex getting himself killed in the war, Pa's dying so unexpectedly and now Ma pregnant. One blow after another.

"After Alex's dying I didn't think there could ever be anything again that would leave me so desolate, so completely helpless."

"Is that what life is, a series of tragedies?" Karl demanded of the darkness around him. "Is life so uncertain we have to live in fear of tomorrow? I never knew there was a harshness to life that could take hold of a family and rip it apart until it was grasping for its very life," Karl told himself, as much in sadness as anger.

He got up from the bench and stood looking across the acres of land that made up the Vokil farm. He knew every inch of this land and every story about its growth from those first few acres his Grandpa bought along with a few trees he liked to call his orchard. One day it was big enough so that Grandpa could give Pa enough land to get a start. Karl had hoped that one day his Grandpa's land would be his.

He walked slowly, his eyes taking in every familiar spot; the oak tree, so immense it shaded the entire yard on hot summer days. Looking up, he could see the bare spot where his Pa had chopped off a couple of dead branches and where he and Alex used to sit and talk. He passed the barn where a restless animal was pounding its hoof in the straw; even in the dim light of evening he could see the neat pile of baskets in the shed. Pa always had them ready for the next year; he went down to the narrow path to the orchard where the bare trees were reminders of the day he and Charlie had stripped the trees of apples and he and his Pa had started out to take them to the cannery.

Karl began to walk aimlessly along the paths, unable to imagine life beyond the farm, until, too weary to think, he slowly retraced his steps back to the house.

Charlie was sitting on the bench waiting for him.

"It's been a sad time for the Vokil's with one shock after another," Charlie began, "but the important thing now is your Ma. We've gotta keep her from doin' any heavy work."

The total impact of his mother's condition was still vague in Karl's mind and the day's events had drained him.

"We can talk about it tomorrow," he told Charlie.

"Sure, sure," Charlie agreed.

Karl went into the house. His mother sat in her rocking chair, a shawl across her shoulders, moving gently back and forth.

"Goodnight Ma," Karl said and started up the stairs, but then, because he knew she had been waiting for him, went back down to sit with her.

Reaching for his hand, she told him, "I've been waiting for you to come in, wondering what was keeping you out there in the dark."

"I guess you could say I'm getting the feel of losing what I thought was always mine," Karl told her, making no attempt to hide his bitterness.

"I don't expect no understanding, Karl, not yet. You think I don't know selling the farm is like cutting a piece of your heart out," she said, "but for me, being alive is more important than a piece of land. One day you'll understand."

Karl let go of his mother's hand and got up. "I don't think so, Ma," he told her. "For me, there's nothing more important than the land." He went up to bed.

11

Next morning when Karl came down, his mother was sitting at the table drinking a cup of tea. Karl poured himself a hearty bowl of porridge, doused it with cream and a large helping of sugar, and sat opposite her. His anger had cooled, but the loss of the farm was like a rock in his belly and not trying to hide his resentment, Karl asked his mother;

"Why did you take Charlie into your confidence and never once mention to me what you were planning?"

"If I'd talked it over with you, son, I knew there'd be no reasoning with you. It was something I had to do, but if you'd known, I knew it would be the end of both of us."

"What do you mean the end of us?" Karl asked.

"I was afraid you'd leave me. Maybe go somewhere where your grandmother's relatives are. I needed to get away from the farm, but I couldn't lose you too."

Karl continued eating his breakfast, thinking about what his mother had said.

"You're right," he admitted. "Something terrible would have happened to us." Alice pored him a cup of tea and made toast for both of them.

"The coals are just right for toast," she told him as she handed him his favorite plum jam. When she sat down again, Karl asked her curtly, "Now that we don't own the farm, where are we gonna live?"

"I bought a small cottage in Farmington, plenty big enough for the two of us." she told him.

Karl sat, brows furled, his dark eyebrows almost meeting, wondering how many more surprises his mother had in store for him.

"And what will we live on?" he asked, knowing she's have an answer for that too.

"I got a fair price for the farm, Karl. There's a goodly amount of land since Grandpa's was added to it."

"I was consoling myself that you were selling the land because without Pa you wouldn't be able to handle the responsibility. I see I was wrong. I'm sure Pa would be surprised to see how fast you've turned our lives upside down, getting rid of everything that was important to the Vokil's, everything we worked so hard for. You and Charlie, going back and forth into town, you taking him, the hired man in your confidence and hiding everything from me." Karl's anger was rising with every word he spoke.

Karl could see by the fury in her eyes, the color of her cheeks, that his mother's anger matched his, but when she spoke, it was in a cold, matter of fact tone.

"Charlie's been a big help to me, driving me where I had to go. After what happened to your Pa, I've been skittish about driving alone. As for my being with child, he knows because he took me to see Doc Hallan. Doc told him having another miscarriage could kill me."

"What do you mean, another miscarriage?" Karl asked.

"There have been others," was all she said.

"Then how come you're having another baby when it could kill you?" Karl asked scornfully.

Alice, hurt by her son's callous attitude, wasn't sure how to answer him. Careful to keep her tone civil, she told him, "You're Pa hoped there'd be more sons, more than just you and Alex. He planned someday owning all the land clear to the new road they're talking of putting in between Farmington and Lockview, but he wanted sons to share it with. Your Grandpa gave your Pa enough land to get a start and your Pa wanted to do the same for his sons."

"Even if having more son's might kill you?" he asked.

"Sometimes when we want something real bad, the consequences are ignored or we convince ourselves nothing bad can happen. It's kinda' the way we are, all of us at times. Even you might find that out when you're older," she added.

Karl knew his mother was making excuses for his Pa and he was somewhat surprised. He knew his Pa's death had been a terrible blow, but that loss had not left her grief stricken or helpless. She had moved quickly, careful to hide her plans from him, knowing that for him there could be no greater tragedy than losing the land. Remembering her condition, Karl felt a pang of guilt at his lack of feeling. He finished is tea and got up from the table.

"I think I'll go out to the orchard and loosen the dirt around the trees," he told his mother. "Even if I don't have a say in what's happening in our lives, I need time to get it all straight in my mind," he said as he reached for his jacket. He was almost out the door when his mother asked him, "Aren't you curious about who bought the land?"

"There's only one man in this county with enough money to buy this land, grab it as fast as you seemed to have sold it, and that's old Pete Grange." Karl snarled. The deliberate cruelness in his tone stunned his mother.

Alice Vokil straightened her back and with her eyes boring into his, she said the one thing that could tear into every fiber of his being, "There's a meanness in you, just like your grandfather," she said.

Karl stood staring at his mother. The color drained from his face, and the eyes, black with rage, frightened her.

Shaken by the terrible anger she had aroused in her son, Alice realized that what she had said could hurt Karl as much as selling the farm. All the years she had kept her feelings about Josuf Vokil to herself, and today she spoke against him to the one person who truly loved him. "For that, he may never forgive me," she thought sadly.

Karl rushed out of the house, letting the door slam behind him. Alice watched as he walked over to the bench and stood looking down at it. He didn't sit down however, but moved in the direction of the path that led to his grandfather's house.

Alice watched until he was out of sight, then went to sit at the table and with her head buried in her arms, she began to cry, loud sobs of regret at the words she had spoken in anger.

Charlie came in to find Alice so distraught she was barely able to talk. He poured her a fresh cup of tea and sat with her. When she told him what she had done, Charlie was amazed that she had stood up to her son and hoped she had given Karl something to think about besides his obsession with the farm.

"It's too much, Charlie," Alice told him, "too many things happening, one on top of the other. I should have talked to him, confided in him, given him the time to get used to the idea before selling the farm."

"He'd never have agreed, not in a hundred years," Charlie told her.

"Maybe not. You're probably right. But selling the farm, it's hurting us both, making us say very cruel things."

And then Alice began to weep again as she hadn't wept since the news of Alex's death. "He's all I've got left, Charlie," she sobbed.

When her crying finally subsided, Charlie convinced her to go upstairs and lie down. "It's not doin' no good, you getting' so upset."

When she had gone upstairs, Charlie went looking for Karl.

Numb with shock, Karl walked slowly towards what had been his grandfather's farm. Trancelike, he followed the path across the field, worn down to dirt from years of use. Once there, he stood looking at the emptiness all around, and felt the quiet, so unnatural on a farm. He let his eyes move from building to building, all empty except the shed where an old wagon with one wheel missing, tipped unsteadily.

The large field that had been Grandpa's garden, and further down, the small orchard, were bleak reminders that life as he and his Grandpa had known it, was ending abruptly. Though he hadn't wanted to, Karl walked over to the house and up the steps until he was standing in the middle of the kitchen, staring at the big black circle where the pot-bellied stove had set. The stout branch Grandpa had used for a cane still leaned against the wall. He turned and left the kitchen, slamming the door behind him.

Instead of rushing home, Karl sat on the step, his mother's words echoing in his ears; "There's a meanness in you, just like your Grandpa."

Karl sat, thinking about what she had said. "A meanness..."

"Is it true?" he asked himself. "Does the land mean so much to me that nothing else matters not even my mother?" Karl immediately thought of his brother, of the way his Grandpa always reminded him that, "he was no Vokil with them blue eyes and hair so light you can't hardly see it. Just like his Ma's."

"Had she suffered too?" he wondered.

"When I think of the land, I think of it as something alive, so responsive to the spring rains and the summer sun, that at harvest time it gives an abundance and nourishes us until the cycle begins again and replenishes the storehouses."

Karl was sure his Grandpa felt the same as him about the land, but did his Grandpa's love extend only to those whose love of the land equaled his?

There had never been a time in his life when Karl had measured his love for his Grandpa against the way his Grandpa treated Alex. The bond had been too tight to allow for thoughts of what his mother called "Grandpa's meanness."

"Is there a meanness in me because of the way I feel about the land?"

Karl continued to sit, thinking about himself and Alex, and he knew his love of the land had never made him act mean to Alex because Alex didn't love the land the way he did. Impatient with his grumbling sometimes, but never mean.

His Grandpa's stories made his life sound so exciting, his long struggle so rewarding.

There were stories about his homeland, and about his Pa and Ma and his brothers who worked in the same fields with him. There were stories about places I'd never see, and about the people who helped him on his long journey on foot to a shipyard where he worked to earn his passage to America.

"Grandpa was telling about a life he'd lived before I was born and doesn't exist anymore. Telling me he was remembering it all, not just for him but for me too."

Life can change so quick, Karl was learning. "In a few years, nobody'll remember my Grandpa, Josuf Vokil, an immigrant from Poland, owned and worked this land, planted fruit trees, a few each year until he had enough to call it an orchard. But I'll remember," Karl told himself.

"And someday I'll tell my children. But does Ma think if I had to make a choice between her and the land, I'd choose the land? That like Grandpa, it's all I can see, nothin' but the land?"

"I don't think so Ma."

"There's no meanness in me, Ma," Karl said with confidence. "It takes time to sort out all that's happened to our family. And I'm not kidding myself thinking that I'm not going to miss the farm something terrible, but I'm not going to be responsible for losing you too!"

Karl got up from the step and took one last look around the deserted farm. Aloud, he told his grandpa, "Grandpa, I always agreed with you, but right now, for Ma and me, the land isn't everything," and he walked the last time along the worn path, away from the life and era that was over.

Charlie saw Karl coming across the field so there was no need to go looking for him. He waited until he was in the yard, then suggested they sit on the bench and have a talk. Karl followed without a word. Charlie gave him a second look, but his face told him nothing.

"Karl, we gotta get your Ma into town so she's near Doc Hallan," Charlie told him with real concern.

Karl nodded in agreement.

"If we get the chores done early, we can start movin' tomorrow, taking what she needs until we're able to empty the house. She'll be near Doc Hallan and this will keep her from doin' any heavy lifting." Charlie looked at Karl for approval but once again he merely nodded in agreement.

With Karl following Charlie's lead, the moving wasn't as bad a Karl expected. They were up early attending to the farm chores and those taken care of, they began packing and loading the wagon. When they got the first load into Farmington, Karl examined the cottage. His Ma was right. It was big enough for two. Other than that, there wasn't much to say, but by the time they'd brought a couple more loads, Karl was surprised at how pleasant his mother was making the cottage.

Curtain covered the windows, a small rug brightened the floor in the parlor. The large kitchen had plenty of shelves for his mother's jellies and jams, and there was room enough for the old kitchen table and chairs, and maybe Ma's sewing machine.

"We'll bring your china cabinet along with your fancy dishes on by themselves so nothing happens to them," Karl told his mother.

Alice felt the loosening of the bitterness inside her son, but wondered about the days ahead when there were no chores to do, no traveling back and forth for their belongings.

When the last load was on the wagon, Karl walked through the empty house, his footsteps loud on the bare floors. There were marks on the wall where their few pictures had hung. It was a sad, dismal sight, its very emptiness reflecting their lives as they were now. They'd have to start building a future, but for the present it was something Karl didn't wanted to think about.

He went out to hitch the wagon and let his eyes roam over the farm one last time, all the way to the piece of land at the end of the lot. "Pa's dream of a vineyard, gone, like everything else." Karl shook off the sense of desolation that was beginning to close in on him, aware that his determination to let go of the farm didn't mean there'd be no feeling of loss, no terrible feeling of emptiness as the only life he'd ever known was now over.

"You comin'?" Charlie hollered.

Karl grabbed the wooden bench and put it on the wagon.

"Why you bringin' that old piece of wood?" Charlie asked. Karl climbed on the wagon without answering.

12

They unloaded the wagon, and Karl went with Charlie to the livery stable to board the one horse they'd need for the buggy. When they came back to the cottage, Alice had a long list for Charlie.

"These are the things that aren't part of the selling price of the farm," she said, handing him the list. "Check it over the two of you, and I'll take it to the lawyer one day soon."

Charlie took the list. "I'll check to see if there's more that should be added. No sense leavin' it for the Granges. Folks say they got more money than brains."

Alice laughed, a lighthearted laugh. Karl looked carefully at his mother. Her blue eyes sparkled. Her hair, the color of white wheat, was pulled back with a pink ribbon. She wore a simple dark dress with a lacey collar and lacey cuffs. Over the dress was a bright, flowery apron that must have hid the baby because you couldn't see any sign that she was pregnant.

Karl was so surprised, he could help blurting out, "Ma, you look beautiful."

Alice gave another lighthearted laugh and smiled at her son. "She enjoys compliments and she's happy to be relieved of the farm," Karl realized. But for him, the thought of the farm brought a pang of regret.

"For now, it doesn't matter," he told himself. "For now, I want everything to be right for Ma."

But it did matter, and everything wasn't alright for Karl. In spite of all his mother had done to make the cottage pleasant, Karl felt boxed in. On either side were other cottages. Out back was a small patch of dirt, hardly big enough for a garden. Looking up he could see a small bit of blue sky, but the big trees hid most of it so's you couldn't see enough to know if the clouds were bringing rain. There was nothing here of the world Karl had known.

Going from a hard-working farm boy to a do-nothing town boy was unbearable. Even as a kid, he and Alex had been up early helping with chores before going off to school. And Pa always had a pile of jobs waiting for them when they got home. Karl never knew there was such a thing as doing nothing all day unless you were real sick or real old.

Karl had deliberately stayed away from the farm, not just missing it, but afraid of what he might see.

"One of these days you ain't gonna recognize the place," Charlie told his Ma and him.

Today the need to see the farm was drawing him like a magnet. Karl strode over to the livery stable, his steps deliberate, so he wouldn't change his mind, saddled his horse and rode out.

Once inside the gate, he reined his horse and sat staring in disbelief. "It's not the Vokil farm no more," he cried out, and raising himself in the stirrups to see beyond the workers, he stared across the field where a pile of rubble was all that was left of Grandpa's house.

Karl sank back, buried his head in the horse's thick mane and wept in quiet despair. The sounds of hammers and saws were like a chant, telling him over and over, "it's not the Vokil farm no more, it's not the Vokil farm no more."

Charlie had been spying on him and hurried over.

"You shouldn't have come Karl," he told him.

Karl lifted his head and nodded.

"How's your Ma?" Charlie asked.

"She's doing alright," Karl answered. "Come and see us,

Charlie," he told him, then turned his horse away from the farm and road out.

Riding home slowly, struggling to accept the changes going on at the farm, Karl told himself, "I got over Grandpa's dying. I managed when I knew Alex wasn't coming home. So far, I've managed without Pa. Time will help. I'll get through this too."

13

The aroma of freshly baked bread greeted Karl as he opened the door of the cottage. He hung his jacket on the peg by the door and went looking for his mother. He found her laying on her bed, face squinted in pain, fear in her eyes. Karl pulled the quilt close around her and told her, "I'll fetch Doc Hallan."

Doc Hallan came quickly. He pulled the quilt to expose blood soaking the sheet under Alice.

"She'd be better off at the hospital," he told Karl, but bouncing over those rough roads for all those miles could make things worse. By the time we got her there, she might be dead."

There were times when, sitting next to his mother as she lay so still, Karl wondered if she was still breathing at all, the fear would come up into his throat almost gagging him and he wondered if they shouldn't have tried getting her to the hospital.

But Doc Hallan came often to see her, and Karl found his visits reassuring. When he came, his visits were leisurely. Karl would take him to his mother's room and he'd talk quietly to her until he knew she was aware of his presence, and he'd wait for her to open her eyes. Then while he examined her, he would continue his conversation, telling her a story or an anecdote, watching her reaction, intent on keeping her alert.

"We don't want her to get discouraged with her loss of pep. It'll come back gradually. Encourage her to take an interest in the world around her," Doc Hallan advised Karl.

Sometimes if there was freshly brewed coffee, Doc Hallan would take a cup down off the shelf, fill it and sit talking to Karl while he drank it.

Karl liked to examine the doctor, more obviously than he realized. Town folk dressed different from farmers. Karl found it hard to believe any one person had so many outfits. Every day a different tie and a freshly starched shirt and sometimes even a different suit. For someone who'd grown up in overalls and a suit of sorts for church and weddings, the fashionable attire of Doc Hallan was new to Karl.

"I guess he's what you call a gentleman," Karl decided. "I bet he gets his mustache clipped at the barber shop and probably his hair too. Too bad he has to wear those heavy glasses. They hide his eyes."

"I'll see if I can find Mrs. Turner to come to help you take care of your mother." Doc Hallan's voice interrupted Karl's scrutiny and he felt his face flush at being caught staring.

"Ma and Mrs. Turner get along good together," he said hastily, trying to hide his embarrassment, "and I sure would appreciate some help."

In the kitchen after the doctor left, trying to water down the oatmeal he'd made so it would be thin enough for his mother to swallow, Karl heard a knock at the door. "Must be Doc Hallan forgot something," he decided as he went to answer it.

"My husband tells me you aren't much of a nurse or a cook," a strange woman told him, handing him a kettle and following him into the kitchen.

"I'm Marge Hallan, the doctor's wife," she said removing her wide brimmed hat and tucking a few wisps of red hair back into place. "You must be Karl." Too surprised to do anything besides take the kettle and nod, Karl stood tongue tied.

"Is it alright if I go in to see your mother?" she asked.

Karl led her to the bedroom. "She hardly moves," he told her.

Marge could hear the worry in his voice and see the weariness and fear in his eyes. "Why don't we see if we can get her to have a little soup I brought.," she suggested. "It's been known to be a kind of cure all."

Not sure what she meant by a "cure all," but glad to have something other than watered down oatmeal to feed his mother, Karl watched as Mrs. Hallan spooned soup to her. "She needs nourishment," Mrs. Hallan told him.

"Try to get her to take a little soup every little while, and be careful it isn't too hot."

"She'll get better won't she?" Karl asked.

Moved by concern in his voice, Marge was quick to try to reassure him. "I have a feeling she's going to be fine. She's survived a lot through the years. She'll come through this," she told him.

"As soon as we can get in touch with Mrs. Turner, we'll send her along," Mrs. Hallan promised Karl as she was leaving.

Mrs. Hallan's visit and the soup had given Karl a temporary boost, but sitting next to his mother through the long hours, watching her lay so still, his mind began to dwell on past tragedies and the loss of the farm. A gentle tap on the door was enough to make him jump.

"It's just me," Doc Hallan said as he poked his head in the room. "How are things today?" he asked.

"Mrs. Hallan was here yesterday and brought soup for Ma and I've been giving it to her. She only takes a few spoonful's at a time," Karl told him.

"In a few days we'll see the roses coming back in her cheeks. Mrs. Hallan's soup has wonderful recuperative powers," the doctor told him.

Karl went to sit in the parlor while Doc Hallan spent time with his mother.

"Your mother's weak but with good care she'll come through this," Doc Hallan assured Karl. "You can keep giving her a little warm soup and talk to her when you're sitting with her. Hearing your voice will reassure her."

"Just like your words reassure me," Karl thought as he walked the doctor to the door.

"Mrs. Turner will be along as soon as she finds the message I tacked to her door," Doc Hallan told him.

Later in the morning, Mrs. Turner came knocking on the door and in no time, she was bustling around, bathing his mother, puffing up her pillows, feeding her soup, and all the while chatting about the goings on in Farmington.

"Doc. Hallan must have given her the same advice he gave me about talking to Ma. She's sure talking the dreariness right out of the cottage," Karl told himself, feeling a sense of relief for the first time. "You'll have Ma better in no time," Karl told Mrs. Turner.

Mrs. Turner put her arm around Karl. "She's not one to give up on life, she told him. A few weeks and she'll be herself again."

To Karl's surprise, Mrs. Hallan came every few days to check on his mother.

The doctor's wife intrigued Karl just as her husband had. She was different from any woman he'd ever known and every time she came, he found himself watching her. She had a head of red curly hair with a wisp always dangling on her forehead and she was constantly trying to tuck it under with a comb or a hair pin.

"It's always been unmanageable," she told Karl when she caught him watching her, but her green eyes twinkled.

She likes having me watch her, Karl decided. It reminded him of the pleased look his mother had given him when he'd told her how nice she looked. Karl was beginning to realize how little he knew about women, and that there was a big difference between a farm woman and a city woman. Mrs. Hallan, for instance, always looked like she was dressed for a ball. The full flowing dresses she wore rustled when she waked. Except for the time she had come with the soup, she always wore gloves and a wide brimmed hat.

Karl even noticed her shoes. They were made of soft leather that sometimes buttoned and sometimes laced up over tiny feet.

"She's not much taller than Ma," Karl decided, "but she moves so sure of herself, you never notice whether she's tall or short." He wondered how old she was, but of course, he knew better than to ask.

Karl took turns with Mrs. Turner, sitting at his mother's side, encouraging her to stay awake, propping her up with pillows so she could look outside. Only the trees were visible, but sometimes a bird would sit on a branch and sing, bringing a smile to his mother's face.

Dozing as he sat with her one afternoon, her hand on his woke him. Surprised, he asked her, "Have you been awake long?"

"Only long enough to know I'm hungry," she told him.

Karl went in search of Mrs. Turner, delighted with his mother's progress, thankful that another tragedy in the Vokil family had been averted.

Mrs. Hallan continued her visits, pleased with Alice's progress, encouraging her to walk in the fresh air, accompanying her the first few times she ventured out. In no time, at her insistence, they were calling her Marge.

It wasn't long before Alice grew impatient with the long days and complained that idleness didn't suit her.

"On the farm there was always more work than there were hours in the day," she told them.

"There's not a lot of places for women to work except taking care of the sick, and you're not up to anything like that, not for a while," Marge told her. But a couple of weeks later, Marge came with news of a job at the bakery.

"Nothing exciting," she told Alice. "Just a few hours a week while Mrs. Carter prepares and delivers the day's orders."

Thrilled, Alice's blue eyes sparkled with pleasure.

"Your mother's bubbling with energy. Has she always been this enthusiastic about life?" Marge asked Karl one day.

"I think she's beginning to enjoy life," Karl answered thoughtfully. "Being a farmer's wife doesn't leave much spare time. During the harvest, when along with the regular chores of fixing meals and baking bread and feeding the pickers, there was always baskets of fruit and vegetables to put down. We never gave much thought to how hard she worked, maybe cause we were so busy ourselves."

"Do you think she misses the farm?" Marge asked him.

Karl didn't answer right off. After thinking it over, he told her, "We don't say much about the farm, Ma and me."

Comparing the two, mother and son, it didn't take much for Marge to see there could have been a problem. Karl was all farmer, from the height and girth of him to the thick, black hair that had never seen a barber. The rough hands were used to cold water and heavy work clothes were probably ordered from a catalogue. His mother, on the other hand, was so small and frail looking. Marge wondered why he hadn't been left to run it. "My husband probably knows." Marge decided she would ask him.

The complete recovery of his mother left Karl stranded with long days of idleness and loneliness. Sitting alone on the bench, his thoughts began returning to the farm. The events that had led to his present situation became uppermost in his mind and watching his mother as she moved about in her new life with a jaunty step, Karl wondered if she ever thought about the farm. Did she ever miss it and Pa. The anger and resentment began to resurface as he wondered what was to become of him. It was Marge who shook him out of his lethargy.

"What are your plans for the future?" she asked him one day while visiting his mother.

"No plans, really," he admitted. "I know I should go back to school, but the school year is almost over and besides, there probably isn't a desk that I could fit my feet under."

"You should talk to Mrs. Gartner, the high school teacher. She's a widow and she might be willing to tutor you after school hours," Marge suggested.

"I don't think I'd be comfortable with a tutor," Karl told her.

"You say you should go back to school but would be uncomfortable in a classroom and don't think you'd be comfortable with a tutor. Are you sure you want an education?" Marge asked in an uppity tone that made Karl bristle.

His dark eyes glaring, Karl told Marge, "Mrs. Gartner was never able to understand why farm boys missed so many school days. Planting and harvesting weren't excuses and her meanness caused lots of boys to quit school."

Karl's outburst surprised Marge. He's not so placid after all. Brooding and unhappy, he's lost without the farm. The bitterness in him is against more than Mrs. Gartner. If he's serious about school, Gary might be able to talk Mitch into tutoring him.

"Dr. Hallan has a friend who might agree to tutor you," Marge told him, intent on steering him away from the resentment he was harboring and back to thinking about this future.

"I can talk to him if you'd like," Marge offered.

"Yea, I guess so," Karl said and it seemed to Marge, that Karl's acceptance was more compliant than eager.

She left the cottage unsure about Karl's desire to finish high school. "I'll talk to Gary," she decided. "He knows him better than I do."

"He's lonely, Marge, and still angry about his mother selling the farm," Gary told her. "Mitch'll shake him up. He won't have time to brood, and getting an education is the best thing for him. I'll talk to Mitch," he promised.

"His name is James Mitchell and he's also a retired teacher," was all Marge told Karl about the man who was to spend the next two years helping him get a high school diploma. Gone were the long hours of idleness, the time spent on the bench brooding over the loss of the farm.

Mitch, as James insisted on being called, was dismayed at the lack of consistency in Karl's schooling.

"I talked to Mrs. Gartner," he told Karl. "She says your attendance was erratic, and that your interest in learning depends on the seasons."

The accusatory tone irritated Karl and he was quick to defend himself. "It's like I told Marge Hallan, Mrs. Gartner drove the boys away from school. She could have helped us catch up when planting and harvesting was over. Instead, she made it sound like we were lazy, skipping school whenever we had a mind to."

Mitch smiled at the memories of trying to help the young farm boys see the importance of school, but with little encouragement from their parents, most quit as soon as they were sixteen and by eighteen, they were married.

"We'll workout a simple schedule until I figure out just what you know," Mitch told Karl, and skeptical of him as a serious student, Mitch mapped out a schedule that required the barest of effort on Karl's part for passing grades. But Mitch, slow to see anything but the farmer in Karl, had misjudged his student. It wasn't long before he realized he had a student whose enthusiasm for learning was boundless.

Karl wasn't sure if he had a real thirst for knowledge or if it was his way of keeping his thoughts off the farm.

Sitting alone on the bench one day after Mitch had left, thinking about the direction his life had taken, Karl realized that learning was pushing thoughts of the farm further away. The need to ride out wasn't strong like it used to be, but he often wondered about the new owners and their feelings for the land. "Do they understand the land the way my Grandpa and I did?" he asked himself. "Will a good harvest make them feel like Pa did when he came in the house with a basket full from the garden and the orchard? Will the land be as important to them as it's bounty?"

"There ain't nothin' like the land…" His Grandpa's words rang in his ears and thinking about strangers owning Vokil land, Karl felt a knot beginning to pull at his insides. He got up off the bench and went indoors to study his lessons.

Late one afternoon, Marge stopped at the cottage.

"Come for dinner," she invited him. "Dr. Hallan and I are anxious to know how school is coming along."

For Karl, this invitation was the start of a relationship with the Hallan's that Karl liked to remind them, help settle his future.

After almost two years of studying with Mitch, the end of their association was nearing as Karl prepared for the last of his exams.

Today, as they sat out on the bench enjoying the late spring weather and Alice Vokil's thick sandwiches along with a cold drink, Mitch wondered about Karl's future. The long association with his grandfather had left little room for normal, social development and with long, summer days ahead, he wondered how Karl would fill the hours now that his studies were complete.

Curious, Mitch asked him, "What are your plans for the summer?"

"No plans," Karl answered.

"No girlfriend to picnic in the park with?" Mitch kidded.

The dark eyes held Mitch's momentarily, surprised at the question, then looked away as he told Mitch, "When I was seventeen, I thought I had a girlfriend."

"Sally and me had been friends in school and I decided I'd like to court her, and when I was eighteen, I figured on marrying her. I planned on asking my Pa if I could fix up my Grandpa's housed and we could live there."

"When I got around to more than just thinking about it, she was being courted by someone else and didn't give me more than a passing glance."

"Eighteen seemed like the magic age. You were a man, all grown, ready to take on the responsibilities of life," Karl said with a wistful, half smile, remembering the confidence he felt as he drove to church that morning.

"And then?" Mitch asked.

"My life changed. The magic of eighteen passed me by without my even noticing it."

There was a weariness in Karl's voice that prompted Mitch to ask Karl, "How old are you?" though he was sure he knew.

"Twenty," Karl told him.

"The magic of eighteen is a fantasy, as you well know, but there is magic in life, Karl," Mitch said in a quiet, contemplative voice.

Karl got up from the bench, and Mitch knew it was Karl's way of ending the conversation. Whatever magic Karl had thought existed, Mitch hoped someday it would be real for him again. He patted his shoulder and told him, "See you Monday."

Karl pushed aside Mitch's ideas on the magic of life, intent on the realities he couldn't push aside.

"Two years of studying with Mitch, and soon I'll have a high school diploma, but still no plans for the future," Karl reminded himself despondently.

Wondering aimlessly into the cottage, Karl looked at the open books on the table, but he's had enough studying for today. He closed the books, put them in a neat pile, and went back out to sit on the bench.

"Perhaps I should back to being a farmer," he told himself, but he knew that life had ended with the selling of the farm. It wasn't just the farm that was gone. It was a way of life that played itself out with tragedy.

Restless, he decided to go for a walk.

Walking had become a habit with Karl. After long hours of study, a brisk walk relaxed him and the village of Farmington became as familiar to him as the cottage he lives in. It hadn't changed much from the days when the family rode into town on Saturdays. The Dieppes still ran the hardware store and the Shieners the grocery store. The empty lot next to Schieners was still a gathering place for the kids, a place to play ball in the summer and a place to skate and play hockey in the winter. But the Schieners didn't live over the store anymore. They'd built a new house outside the village and Karl passed it often on his walks.

Mrs. Moore's fabric shop was still the gathering place for the women, where they'd get caught up on the latest gossip.

Sometimes Karl stopped at the little ice cream parlor for a cone, but most of the time he preferred to circle the village, to walk along the dusty roads where there were wild flowers growing in the grassy fields. One day when he was out walking, Karl discovered a patch of wild strawberries hidden on the edge of a small glade. He couldn't remember ever having tasted anything so sweet and took off his cap and picked until it was full. His mother had laughed.

"It's not likely you'll wear this cap again," she told him, but they had a feast of wild strawberries that night.

Karl knew where the bulrushes grew tallest and had cut some with his jackknife for Mrs. Carmody, who often stopped him on his walks and invited him in for a cold drink and a few cookies. Today, the brisk walk was neither relaxing nor helpful.

"What I need is someone to talk to, someone to help me make a decision." "Marge usually has a headful of ideas," Karl told himself and decided to stop and talk to her.

Marge's friendship had become important to Karl. Once he had started his studies, they had more to talk about and she encouraged him to come and examine the book shelves, to see if there was something he'd like to read. From the beginning, Karl had been drawn to the stacks of medical journals. They were a change from the list of books Mitch insisted he read and found the information new and interesting.

"Those books go back to the days when Doc Hallan had his

office in the house. They're pretty old," Marge told Karl. Karl didn't mind. The old journals held a whole world of information he knew nothing about. "I always thought measles was measles, but some are worse than others," Karl discovered. He knew about germs but virus was a new term to him.

Once Karl realized how little he knew, he poured over Doc Hallan's journals. He'd take a couple home and hide them in his bureau drawer so Mitch wouldn't see them and get on him about spending his time reading material that wasn't part of his schooling.

Today, Marge greeted Karl warmly, as always, chatting as she led him into the parlor where he was soon eyeing the book shelves. "Same old journals," she told him.

"Some of those journals must go back to the Dark Ages," Karl told her as he sorted through them.

"I don't think so, but they'd be pretty interesting if they did, don't you think?" Marge said.

Thumbing through a journal and without looking up, Karl asked her, "Did you know my brother wanted to be a doctor?"

"Your mother told me about him. I'm sorry Karl," Marge said, watching him curiously. He'd never mentioned his brother before today.

"Pa never understood. Not to love the land. We were all like that, Grandpa, Pa and me," Karl admitted.

Marge heard the bitterness in his voice and wondered if it wouldn't be good for Karl to talk about his brother and the farm instead of holding it all tight inside himself.

"Your mother told me how angry you were when she sold the farm," she told him, and for the first time Karl let her see a little of the pain that had been part of his life.

"Terrible things were happening to our family. Grandpa, Alex and Pa. all dead, and Ma selling the farm. I couldn't believe she'd do such a thing, not when she knew how important the land was to the Vokils, to me. When she told me she'd sold the farm, if the earth had swallowed me up, I wouldn't have been surprised."

"You should've known my Grandpa," Karl continued, "listened to him tell about his dream to own a piece of land, all his own. He worked a long time to save enough money to buy a piece of land." Karl hesitated, then, explaining his own feelings, he told Marge, "After listening and working with him all those years, of course there was no life for me but the farm."

Marge had never heard Karl talk about the farm or his grandfather with such emotion, and she realized that the haunted look in the dark eyes, the loneliness that was always a part of him were the result of having lost all that was dear to him. His mother had given her the bare outlines of Karl's anger, nothing about his love of the land or his grandfather.

Marge was at a loss as to what to say. Finally, she asked him, "You have found life outside the farm, haven't you?"

"Yea, I have," Karl admitted. "Life on the farm recedes a little more each day, but there has to be something to replace it. It's the future, not the past, I'm wrestling with these days."

"Have you discussed it with Mitch?" Marge asked.

"Right now, Mitch' biggest concern is my exams and my high school diploma," Karl told her.

"Perhaps you need to get away from the books for a while, be with people, learn about all that's going on in the world around you," Marge suggested. "It might help you decide what you'd like to do, then added, "You lead a very lonely life, Karl."

Marge saw the dark eyes glaring at her. He hadn't come to be reminded of his solitary life and it wasn't Marge's place to remind him about it. Not today when he was in such a serious mood, looking for help.

"All I'm saying, Karl, is there's life beyond your cottage and Farmington. It's hard to make a decision about your future when your experience is limited."

Marge waited until the fierceness was gone from his eyes, then told him, "I do have a suggestion, one I've thought about quite often over the past few months," and watching for his reaction, she asked him, "Have you ever thought you might like to be a doctor?" She couldn't tell if her suggestion had surprised him or not.

"Did my telling you about my brother give you that idea?" Karl asked.

"Your interest in my husband's medical journals gave me the idea," she told him. "You always seem to enjoy them more than the books I gave you to read. Sometimes I wondered if your visits were to read journals, not to see me."

Karl grinned and told her, "Probably a bit of both."

Marge sat waiting for him to say more, but he seemed barely aware of her presence as he sat thinking and she realized he probably wouldn't give her an answer without further thought.

"Talk to Doc Hallan. Go with him to the city hospital. Walk along the halls, peek into the rooms, see what impressions you get," Marge suggested.

"You really think I'm smart enough to be a doctor?" Karl asked.

"Of course, you are. I wouldn't mention it unless I thought so. But there's more to being a doctor than being smart, Karl," Marge assured him. There are qualities that are important and will stop you from being a good doctor if you lack them. You'll have to decide if you have those qualities."

Impressed with Marge's seriousness, Karl realized this was something she had been thinking about and he wondered as he often did, why she took such an interest in him. Was it because she never had a child of her own? He didn't think so. He often thought she rescued him from the emptiness of his life simply because it pleased her to, the same as she did for his mother. Once she realized he took learning seriously and enjoyed it, they became friends. He shouldn't be surprised that she was worrying about his future.

"A doctor… I like the idea…" Karl decided, but he needed more

time to think about it. He wanted to talk to Doc Hallan and his
mother.

Marge sat watching him, wondering what he was thinking.
"He's always hard to read, the dark eyes hiding his thoughts.
Sometimes he'd open up and tell me enough so I understood the
sadness that is so much a part of him. Today, when he talked
about his brother and his grandfather, I'd have liked to put my
arms around him, but he'd have pushed me away. I doubt anyone ever comforted him. He'd have been embarrassed if I'd tried.
He'll make a good doctor. He knows about pain and heartache.
But not about love, other than his grandfather's, that is. One day
that'll change, but not soon," she hoped. For now, Marge thought
of him as belonging to her. From farmer to scholar to doctor. "I'm
responsible for that."

Marge then realized Karl was talking to her.

"The idea of being a doctor interests me," he told her. "It's a
challenge to be something that's important to people's lives. I need
to think about this," he said, as he got up to leave.

Marge walked him to the door and stood watching him until he
turned the corner and was out of sight. Slowly, she closed the door
and wondered out to the kitchen to sit alone at the kitchen table,
to think about Karl's visit and how he'd become important to her.

"When he first visited, we always sat in the parlor. Karl was
never really comfortable until he started exploring the bookshelves
and found Gary's journals. Then he'd forget I was there. I'd fix iced
tea and invite him to the kitchen where we'd visit while he emptied
the cookie plate, and I learned how intelligent he was."

Marge found sitting alone at the kitchen table suited her moods.
She could look at the old maple tree in the yard where a brisk wind
rattling the leaves barely interrupted her thoughts.

"I've become a loner," she said, shaking her head at the thought
of how she used to be known as Doc Hallan's gad about wife. "I
loved to take an early train into the city, meet Sal or Jesse or both,

shop until our feet hurt and we were starving, then go to the Saginaw Hotel for lunch where the waiter treated us like royalty. Gary said it was because our tips probably fed his family until the next time we came."

But Sal got pregnant and then pregnant again and none of her clothes fit her and she complained of looking and feeling like a bloated whale.

"Saginaw lunches have gone the way of my twenty-inch waist," she lamented.

"When Jesse and I went shopping for the latest fashions, it was no longer exciting. Sal had been the one to model the newest styles, amusing the clerks and customers alike. And a new waiter at the Saginaw was indifferent to us. Even the food had lost its flavor. Sal's having babies propelled us into a new era where shopping sprees and lunch at the Saginaw were for the younger crowd."

"Before long it was Jesse's turn to get pregnant and we waited for my turn to come around. It didn't."

"I didn't tell Gary I'd gone to see a specialist and been told what I suspected all along."

"No children for you, young lady," he'd said. "He was so casual, so unconcerned with what his words would do to my life. I dreaded telling Gary. He never lost his optimism."

"You're only twenty-seven… you're not thirty yet."

"When I told him we we'd never have children, I knew from the look on his face, I'd pretty much settled my fate. Gary tried to reassure me, but I'd seen the sadness and disappointment in his eyes. I never thought a lot about how my bareness would affect Gary beyond the disappointment, but I was so sure he'd be able to handle it. It just never occurred to me how much it would affect our marriage."

"We were friends, but no longer lovers. Making love would remind both of us that I was barren."

"We went on with the routine of our lives, as though nothing had changed. Gary came home and talked about his day, his patients and their quirks. We argued over politics and the latest fads. We still laughed when we read the Sunday funnies. There are so many things we take for granted. Love, marriage, motherhood, all in their proper order. When one important part is missing, an entire life is suddenly twisted out of shape. I was ready for the Vokil's when Gary sent me on my mission of mercy."

"From the beginning there was something about Karl that intrigued me. His haunted look; his piercing, black eyes. But the haunted look is disappearing. Only the mention of Alex brings it back."

"Karl and Gary get along fine. Gary will be excited about the idea of Karl becoming a doctor. Maybe some day they'll be associates. It'll give Gary something to look forward to."

"For now, I want to watch the changes in Karl when he comes in contact with others his age, when he makes friends and learns that tragedy has more lives than his. I want to hang on to the closeness we have for a while yet."

Walking home slowly, Karl was forced to ask himself if the idea of being a doctor was so appealing because of Alex. "Do I think I can compensate for the tragedy of his life by becoming a doctor? Why was I so interested in Doc Hallan's journals? Was Marge's suggestion what I'd been hoping for when I went seeking her help?"

Suddenly, Karl was tired of the way he allowed his thoughts to seesaw between the past and his future.

"Why did I need Marge to tell me what I've know for a long time. What if my decision was influenced by my brother's death? I only know I haven't felt so excited since the Sunday morning I went to church figuring on asking Sally Reif if I could court her."

Karl stepped up his pace as he hurried home, anxious to tell his mother of his decision.

The following day when Karl was walking around the village, he noticed Doc Hallan's buggy parked in front of the Newton house. He slowed his pace and retraced his steps until, bag in hand, the doctor came out and spied Karl.

"Jump in, Young man," he invited Karl, sure their meeting was more than a coincidence. When they were settled in the buggy, Dr. Hallan told Karl, "I understand you're thinking of med school this fall. It's been a long road for you from the lad who moved into the cottage a couple of years ago."

"It's a different world, alright," Karl admitted. "I guess I find it as hard to believe as you do."

"Once you set your mind on getting an education, the direction of your life changed. But don't rush into this doctor bit, Karl. Medicine is a very demanding profession, and it takes years of hard work to get there."

"Can I give you a word of advice?" the doctor asked, and Karl, pleased with Doc Hallan's interest, told him, "I'd appreciate it."

"Give yourself breathing room. Take a few Pre-Med courses, but keep an open mind," Doc Hallan advised. "If you decide it's not for you, there are other avenues open. Pharmacology, research, x-ray. There's a whole world out there Karl. Take your time. Explore it."

"I'm pretty excited about the idea of being a doctor," Karl told him. "All the worrying about my future is suddenly gone," Karl said with an enthusiasm that surprised the doctor.

"You're that sure?" he asked.

"I think so," Karl told him.

"By the time you graduate, I'll be a few years older, and I'll need some help. The county's growing faster than I'll be able to take care of all the sick." Dr. Hallan looked directly at Karl, "Nothing binding son, but, something to think about a few years down the line."

And then, "whoa," he said to the horse and told Karl, "I'm not going in your direction, but I know you enjoy a good walk."

Karl hardly knew what to say. "I'll think about what you said, and thanks," He said as he jumped down off the buggy.

For a moment before he turned the buggy away, Gary Hallan watched Karl as he strode down the road.

"He's been good for Marge," Gary told himself. "When I mentioned the Vokil's dire circumstances, little did I dream how it would change her life. But how will his going away to college affect her?" Gary realized he was dreading the years ahead when Karl would be away. But even if he wasn't going away to college, he'd outgrow his need for her. "I never could convince Marge that not having children hadn't changed the way I felt about her, that there was a world of difference between disappointment and rejection."

Gary turned the buggy in the direction of his patient, forcing his thoughts away from his own life, to the sick who depended on him.

14

Karl needed only to open the cottage door to know that Marcus, his mother's beau was in the house. The smell of pipe tobacco announced his presence. A rather pleasant smell, Karl decided once he got used to it. He had considered taking up the habit himself until he saw that Marcus spent more time lighting and relighting the pipe than smoking it.

Having Marcus come to court his mother took getting used to, but it took even longer for Karl to get used to walking in the parlor and seeing Marcus sitting in his father's favorite chair.

Karl remembered when his mother had given him the first clue that she had a beau.

Sitting out on the bench with him one evening, she told him. "I'm inviting someone special to dinner Sunday next. His name is Marcus Dole. He's a part-time coroner and an undertaker and works with Doc Hallan a lot. I met him through friends at the Presbyterian Church. I hope you'll like him."

Karl smiled at the matter of fact run down, all the information in a few short sentences. He thought of the day she had told him she had sold the farm. No preliminaries. A rather cryptic statement that left no doubts as to her plans. And now in the same manner, she told him she was being courted, obviously with the intention of remarrying. The idea of his mother marrying had never occurred to Karl and curiosity had him sitting with one eye on the clock and one eye on the window, waiting for Sunday services to be over so he could get a quick look at the man who had captured his mother's interest and maybe her heart.

They came up the short path, Alice with her arm through his, chattering happily as Marcus gazed down at her, smiling, nodding his head, acknowledging or agreeing, Karl didn't know which, but it was there, that special something between them. Karl remembered Mitch telling him, there is magic in life. "Could it be so, at their age," he wondered?

The greeting between the two men was a mixture of curiosity and friendliness as they shook hands then followed Alice into the parlor where Karl had his first shock as Marcus settled himself in Pa's chair.

"You two men get acquainted while I fix dinner, Alice told them as she went into the kitchen. While the pipe smoke swirled around as Marcus lit and relit his pipe, Karl studied him.

He had been looking for a somber, ponderous man, his idea of an undertaker, but there was nothing in Marcus's appearance or manner to indicate the nature of his work. In fact, Karl noticed immediately, that in many ways, Marcus reminded him of Doc Hallan. They were both tall and slim, wore suits that did not come out of the catalog and their stiffly starched shirts were brightened with fancy silk ties.

Marcus was probably a regular at the barber shop, but he was clean shaven and his intelligent grey eyes weren't hidden behind thick glasses.

Marcus asked Karl about his studies, about Mitch and at dinner they talked about Karl's plans to be a doctor.

"I never expected to be anything other than a farmer," Karl told Marcus.

"Sometimes fate has a way of stepping in and taking charge, without the slightest concern for what it does to boyhood dreams," Marcus told Karl. "I always dreamed of being an engineer on the railroad. I'd watched the trains as they chugged into the station, and I saw myself sitting on that seat, pulling the whistle cord, and taking the train to far away exotic places."

"It's a far cry from a railroad engineer to an undertaker, wouldn't you say?" Marcus asked.

Not that much further than from a farmer to doctor," Karl told him.

Marcus chuckled. "Well, let's not tempt fate by admitting to its capriciousness. However, I believe I'd have found being an engineer a bit boring. I make sure I'm equipped with plenty of reading material when I go on a train."

"I don't think I'd be bored," Karl said. "When you've never been more than twenty miles from Farmington, there must be a lot to see. My Grandpa used to tell me about his trips from one end of the Erie Canal to the other, and I've always wanted to see the country he saw."

"The country your Grandfather saw no longer exists Karl," Marcus told him, "but just to travel along the route he traveled and see how different it is from what he saw, I'm sure you'd enjoy it."

After dinner they went to sit on the parlor and enjoy the tea Alice served them. Karl listened to his mother as she discussed the morning services.

"I think sometimes the new pastor is so intent on impressing us with his oratory he forgets to put any meat in is sermons."

Marcus puffed on his pipe, an amused look on his face. "Your mother goes to church to learn about the almighty, but I don't mind a little showmanship thrown in. Keep's you awake."

It was that kind of afternoon, with light, pleasant conversation that gave Karl and Marcus the opportunity to get acquainted, and for Karl, an occasional touch of resentment as he realized his mother had no regrets about selling the farm. But Karl, now that he'd made a decision about his own future was not going to allow himself to let his inner feelings interfere with either his mother's future or his own.

Once Karl told Mitch about his decision to be a doctor, Mitch told him, "You'll have to decide on a college so we can send out applications. I was going to suggest you pick a college close to home. Western New York has some of the best colleges in the state."

"I want to talk to Doc Hallan and Marge too, before I decide," Karl told him.

At dinner, Karl told his mother, "You make one decision and next thing you know there's a whole list of other decisions to make."

She nodded in agreement. "When you're making an important move, there are always decisions to make. I've made a few and want to talk them over with you." She told him.

"You're going to tell me that you and Marcus are going to get married, aren't you?"

"Yes, but you already know that, I'm sure. There are other things I've been meaning to talk to you about. But first, I have a question, about the farm. I need to know how you feel about me selling it. Have you understood enough to forgive me?"

"I understand your reasons for selling it, Ma" Karl assured her, "but I've often wondered if you have any good memories of your life on the farm."

"For me, there was my relationship with Grandpa and my love of farm life. But you and Alex, I always knew how Alex felt, but you, Ma I never thought, not for a minute, about you hating the farm."

"You're only half right about my being unhappy on the farm, Karl," she told him. "I was content on the farm until I wasn't able to give your Pa the sons he'd have liked. With each miscarriage the strength was sapped out of me. Your Grandpa didn't like your Pa marrying me. He didn't like my blue eyes and light hair, and he turned away from me and Alex when he saw Alex looked like me. But you were a true Vokil, and he let me be after you were born."

"Your Pa was disappointed but he didn't treat me bad. But there was Alex." Alice put her head down on the table and let the tears come. His death would be a sadness that would always be there, and Karl, understanding, feeling the loss, waited quietly until she wiped her eyes and continued.

"When your Pa was killed and Doc Hallan told me how bad another miscarriage could be, I made up my mind there was no staying on the farm, waiting to die and I'd take all the hate you have for me when I told you what I'd done."

There was no apologizing, no tears, only her back ramrod straight, that told Karl his mother had no regrets.

It was moments like this that allowed Karl to get a glimpse of a past he hadn't known. His world had been me and grandpa and the land, but the cracks in the Grandpa he'd worshipped were getting wider as Karl realized that the courage and determination that had brought his Grandpa to this land were not excuses for his love-hate relationships, and that there was as much courage in blue eyed blonds as the rugged descendants of Turks and Magyars.

"We Vokil's never learned to look beyond the black, fertile earth," Karl told his mother. "As for forgiving, I wondered if I ever would, but like I told Marge, there is life beyond the farm, for both of us."

"I'm happy you're marrying Marcus, Ma," he continued, "happy you had the courage to sell the farm and have time left for happiness."

Alice's blue eyes had been intent on every word her son said, and now that she was sure there was no longer any resentment between them, she reached over and squeezed his hand, and said, "Let's get these other things taken care of."

She was all business. I talked to Mr. Gargon, the lawyer and had him put the cottage in your name. I always intended that we share the money from the farm. I've put most of it in your name."

Karl started to object, but Alice held up her hand to silence him. "I've talked this over with Marcus. He's not a poor man and there's just the two of us. This is the way it should be. You need a place to call home and money for college."

Karl couldn't help but remember when he'd thought his mother was too overwrought to act responsibly and how she'd surprised him. Here she was surprising him again. Everything all thought out and taken care of.

"Thanks, Ma," he told her, then reminded her, "be sure you let me know the wedding date in time to get a new suit. I want to look my best when I walk you down the aisle."

"I was going to mention the suit, Karl. Not one out of the catalog, please," she said, half joking but serious too. "Now I have to get ready," she said, getting up from the table. "Marcus is coming by for me and we're going over to Roches to play cards. I'm getting pretty good at whist," she told him proudly.

Karl waited until Marcus came by for his mother, then went to sit out on the bench. The cool evening air felt good and there were things to think about. His mother! What a spunky woman she was. "Would Pa recognize her? For sure, Grandpa wouldn't approve," Karl smiled.

The lovely wheat color hair, knotted low on her neck, held by a ribbon on a wide barrette wasn't like Ma on the farm when she was too hot and too busy to worry about how she looked. And now she wore dresses as pretty as Marge Hallan's. It was hard for Karl to believe there were two worlds so different from each other, each capable of bringing happiness as well as tragedy.

For now, the world of Farmington, though only a few miles from the farm, was showing Karl and his Ma its bright side, full of promise for the years ahead. Karl remembered how Marcus had talked about the capriciousness of fate and felt his confidence wobble a little, but not enough to let the past loom up to spoil his plans for the future.

"Have you made a decision about college?" Mitch asked Karl.

"As I told you, there are good colleges in Western New York, so I don't see the need to be sending applications all over the state."

"I'm no authority on colleges near or far," Alice Vokil told her son, "but it seems reasonable to go close to home if you can."

Marcus agreed. "The Pre-Med and Medical Schools nearby are excellent," he told him.

Doc Hallan told him, "Go as far from Farmington as you want, Karl. Just make sure you come back," and he repeated the offer he's made in the buggy. "I'd be happy to have you back, Karl," Doc Hallan told him, "happy to have you hang a shingle next to mine, but don't go away with the idea that you're under any obligation to me or Farmington. By the time you graduate, Farmington may be nothing but a distant memory."

"This is my home," Karl reminded Doc Hallan. "If you still want me and if I make the grade, I'll be happy to take you up on your offer."

"You'll be surprised how exciting college is," Marge must have told him a dozen times, and Karl could feel the excitement building, a little more every day as his future plans began to fall into place.

"Karl, have you picked up your suit at the tailors?" his mother asked him and he had to admit he hadn't. Exams had been on his mind and his mother's wedding had seemed weeks away. "I'll do it this afternoon," he replied.

Meanwhile the commotion at the cottage was too much for Mitch, as friends kept stopping by to help Alice with her wedding preparations.

"How are we supposed to get any work done?" he grumbled.

"Let's take the book's outside," Karl suggested, but the breeze ruffled the papers as well as Mitch's disposition. He stacked his and told Karl, "I'll be back after the wedding."

Relieved to see Mitch leave, Karl went to pick up his suit, the first one that hadn't come out of the catalogue.

Marcus had encouraged him to have it tailor made, and now, trying it on, the tailor hovering over him, checking it for fit and proper length. Karl was amazed at the person he saw in the mirror. He examined himself from every angle, front, back, sides. He buttoned and unbuttoned the suit coat, and delighted with his appearance, couldn't wait to walk his mother down the aisle.

It was a beautiful day for a wedding. The sun shone in a cloudless sky and a gentle breeze floated into the church through open windows.

Walking down the aisle to the soft strains of the wedding march was a woman very different from the one he'd helped nurse back to health. Karl smiled down at her as she tucked her arm in his.

Her blue, silk dress matched the blue of her eyes and swished as she made her way up the aisle. Her light golden hair, coiled up on top of her head, was held in place by a wreath of baby's breath. Her face glowed with happiness.

Marcus, waiting to welcome her, watched her progress up the aisle, smiling happily.

They were a handsome pair, and the small church rang with good wishes for the happy couple.

15

Alone at the cottage now that his mother was married, Karl waited impatiently for the weeks to pass when he'd be off to college. He had taken the advice of Mitch and Marcus and had chosen and was accepted at the University of Buffalo.

When, at last he boarded the train and waved goodbye to his mother, Marcus and Marge, he felt a little like an explorer on his first voyage, apprehensive about the unknown, but at the same time, confident of his ability to reach his destination.

The excitement of a new college year was everywhere, old friends shouting greetings at one another, freshmen milling around in a daze, the campus alive with students weighted down with suitcases and books on their way to their dorm. Such an atmosphere greeted Karl, and though he didn't know a soul, he shared the excitement of that first day.

Karl's roommate, already trying to bring order to the chaos he'd created as he unpacked, greeted him with an apologetic smile and a warm handshake.

"Aaron Noble," he said.

"Karl Vokil," Karl said.

"Where you from?" Aaron asked as he went back to unpacking.

"Farmington," Karl told him and drew a blank look from his roommate.

"It's a small town about twenty miles north of Niagara Falls and not much further from Buffalo," Karl informed Aaron.

"I'm from Hills Park," Aaron said and it was now Karl's turn to draw a blank.

Aaron laughed. "It's half way to Syracuse, dairy farming country," he told him, then asked, "What courses you taking?"

"Pre-Med," Karl answered. "And you?" he asked.

Aaron, a math and physics major, was into courses that Karl was ashamed to admit, he knew little about, but that didn't interfere with their becoming friends.

The daily routine of each day helped Karl adjust to college life and eventually feel comfortable with his classmates. As he made his way across the campus to his first class, he crossed paths with the same students every morning.

By mid-semester there, the morning greeting had progressed from a curt nod to a friendly hello to an exchange of trivia and finally their names.

After having studied alone for two years, Karl found classroom instruction exciting, the interchange between professor and student a natural outlet for his enthusiasm about everything he was learning.

It was an exciting year.

One morning Karl and Aaron awoke to the realization that their freshmen year was over, that it was time to pack and head for home, and the refrain, "see you all in the fall," echoed through the halls.

Packed and ready to go home for summer break, Karl stood alone at the window after Aaron had left, watching the activity on campus. "The scene is the same," he told himself with a wry smile. Students milling around, suitcases and books on the ground, a cacophony of sounds. But it's goodbyes this time. A whole year has passed.

"How many have changed as much as I have?" Karl wondered.

"My scholastic achievements would please even Mitch, but I've learned more than what's in the books. I've made friends and experienced the warmth of companionship and forgot about my loneliness. My world is expanding beyond the small town of Farmington."

Karl smiled as he picked up his suitcase. "Marge was right when she said I'd love college," he told himself as he went to join the group below.

16

Marcus came with his mother to meet him at the station.

"It'll be good to have you around for more than a weekend," his mother said. "I've missed you."

They dropped him off at the cottage.

"Your welcome to stay with us," Marcus offered, as he did each time Karl came home.

"I'll come to dinner, but the cottage is home to me," Karl said as he and Marcus took his bags in. Once settled, Karl went in search of the Hallan's.

"You're finally home." Marge was all smiles as she greeted him with a hug and led him into the parlor. "Tell me about your exams and how you and Aaron celebrated when they were over," Marge asked.

"There's not a lot to tell," Karl told her. "Exciting as it was, it's not something you can put into words."

"You'll come for dinner, won't you?" Marge invited. "Gary will be happy to see you."

"I'll stop by later in the evening," Karl promised. "I told my mother I'd have dinner with them."

Karl enjoyed the first couple of weeks of relaxation, not having to worry about studying or exams. He enjoyed the visits with his mother and Marcus and with the Hallan's, but was surprised at how quickly the conversation lagged.

He sat on the bench, reading Doc Hallan's journals, and found some of the articles interesting now that he had a little knowledge under his belt. But the reading was mostly a way of putting in time and when he closed the book and sat looking off into the distance, it was the farm he saw.

Memories came flooding back. "It's fruit picking time, Pa always roamed the orchard, checking the fruit to make sure it was just right before letting the workers in to pick. We were busy from sun up to sun down and always, at the end of the day, I went over to sit with Grandpa."

"At college, thoughts of the farm weren't on my mind long enough to bring back sad memories." He got up off the bench and went into the house to check the calendar and count the days until it was time to go back to school.

The first person Karl met as he was lugging his suitcases to his room was Aaron. They dropped their bags long enough to give each other a bear hug and a warm handshake.

"Another year of suffering," Aaron moaned. "we're roommates again," and laughing, excited about being back at school, they dropped their belongings in their rooms and went in search of familiar faces and old friends.

Julia Ekhart, one of the few women students, greeted Karl with open arms. "You can't believe how happy I am to see you!" she squealed.

"Classes haven't started yet and you're already making sure there's someone around to help you with your labs," Karl accused her.

Julia laughed. "True enough," she admitted, "but I'm glad to see you even if you never help me with another lab."

Julia's welcome gave him a sensation that was new to him, a kind of shaking inside. Karl felt his excitement rise as he contemplated the year ahead.

In no time, they were back in the routine of classes, rushing across the campus, stopping for short chats with old friends and Karl helping Julia with her labs.

"It's an exciting year," Karl told the Hallan's when he visited home one weekend. "I've learned to relax and enjoy what free time I have. Julia still depends on me to help her with her labs and we've become good friends. My classes and labs are getting more interesting all the time."

"Aaron has invited me to visit his family over the holidays. Did I tell you they are dairy farmers?" Karl talked non-stop and when he ended his conversation by enthusiastically telling them, "I didn't think the second year could be more exciting than the first." Marge gave her husband a long, thoughtful look. Later after Karl had gone home, she told her husband, "He's changed, hasn't he? Do you think we're losing him?" she asked concerned.

"It's too soon to tell," he told her. "He's having what you call a first fling, the time of his life. It'll be a while before he knows what he wants to do. We'll have to wait and see."

Gary found the changes in Karl a healthy sign, but he worried about Marge. Will she be able to handle the changes, accept them? Or will she feel rejected a second time? The thought disturbed him.

"I think I'll walk over to the hotel, see if the boys have the world situation in hand," Gary told Marge.

"Damn prohibition," he muttered as he walked toward the hotel. "What I need is a good shot of bourbon."

Alone after her husband left, Marge sat thinking about Karl. "He smiles so easily, is enjoying college life, not missing Farmington. Is he planning on a future different from what Gary had hoped for?" She asked herself. And had to agree with her husband... "We'll have to wait and see. He still had a long way to go."

17

By the end of his third year, Karl was asking himself if Doc Hallan was right when he said Farmington might end up no more than a memory. But he chose to put that thought aside. "It's still too soon to make a serious decision about the that part of my future," he told himself. But alone in the cottage, he realized how lonely he was, and how he missed, not only Aaron and Julia, but other friends and acquaintances along with the busy college atmosphere.

As he sat with the Hallan's one evening after a long lonely day, Karl began to reminisce out loud about his college year.

"My visits home with Aaron were the times I enjoyed the most," he told himself. "Someday I'd like to have a family like the Nobles; warm, caring and happy."

"Aaron and his family laughed at my interest in the country-side. Rolling hills and vast green pastures where hundreds of cows grazed, were sights that fascinated me. Do you realize I'd never been more than twenty miles from Farmington and would you believe Aaron's father tried to interest me in becoming a vet?"

Karl barely stopped for a breath as he went on to talk about Julia. "She's a med student who's been in all my labs since the beginning. She depends on me for help. I guess I've mentioned her before."

Marge nodded yes, aware there was a warmth to their relationship that hadn't been there a year ago.

"Julia is hoping we can intern in the same hospital, but her father's a surgeon in Syracuse. I imagine that's where he'll insist she go. They invited me out to dinner one evening when Dr. Ekhart was in Buffalo," Karl continued, unaware of the stir he was causing. "He said almost every area in his part of the state is looking for young doctors."

As Karl related these events of his year, the pattern he wove was one a world that was slowly leading him away from Farmington. As the Hallan's listened, and exchanged worried glances, they could only wonder what the next year would do to unravel their hopes.

"Have we lost him Gary?" Marge asked her husband.

"He still has a way to go," Gary reminded her.

With time on his hands, Karl fell into his old habit of walking, sometimes, as today, starting out in the early morning hours when he could enjoy the fresh smell of morning air and when the dew still glistened on the grass. There was a quietness that belonged only to this time of day. It held a feeling of peace and tranquility as most of the town still slept, not yet concerned with the cares of another day.

As Karl skirted the town, he realized that even at this early hour, he was hearing sounds of activity somewhere off in the distance. Curiosity made him quicken his pace as he neared the park that bordered the town, he spied a Ferris wheel and recognized the activity as part of the preparation for the summer fair. A group of men were putting together stands and bleachers. Karl went over and began carrying the heavy planks to the men equipped with hammers and saws. They handed him a hammer and nails with the invitation to join them. The day turned into one of hard physical work, more than Karl had done since leaving the farm, but as he worked side by side with the townspeople, there was no loneliness to shake off. As they parted at the end of the day, it was with a warm handshake and greeting, "see you at the fair."

Karl stood alone after the others had gone, looking at what was now the fair grounds. As the Ferris wheel cast its shadow across the grounds, its empty seats bobbing in the breeze, and the tiers of bleachers they had put together were ready to be filled by half the county by noon tomorrow, Karl was remembering the last time he had been at the fair.

"A long time ago," he thought with a touch of nostalgia, remembering when the Volkil's were a family and when Alex and he shared the fun of those days. But tonight, in spite of the sad memories, Karl realized that the loner he had been was slowly disappearing and that he was looking forward to tomorrow and the fair.

Karl awoke the next morning with the same feeling of anticipation he had experienced the night before and was anxious to join the throngs he knew would be at the fair.

Almost immediately, he met up with Sally and Pete Korda, a young lad holding his father's hand and Sally heavy with a second child.

They greeted him warmly, and Karl had a momentary feeling of regret as he looked at Sally's lovely, smiling face.

There were others. The Hawthorne's, Steve, Alex's best friend and his wife, Jenny. Steve's firm handshake, holding Karl's hand for a few extra seconds, was a reminder of the loss they shared. The Wieppes and Morgan's stopped, anxious to reminisce about their school days, curious about Karl's plans.

Like the rest of his schoolmates, they were married, with young one's tagging along.

Jed Gargon, son of Farmington's only lawyer, greeted him with a slap on the back and a broad smile.

"My dad said we'll soon have two doctors in Farmington," he told Karl.

"Not for a couple of years yet," Karl said. "And how is the next lawyer-to-be?" he asked.

"Struggling," Jed admitted. "If you recall, I was never the smartest kid in class."

Karl laughed. "Mrs. Gartner always seemed to believe all your excuses for not having your homework done. Did you know we all thought you were the teacher's pet?"

"Did you know that Mrs. Gartner was an old flame of my father's," Jed confided. "How else would I'd have gotten out of high school?" he joked.

"Are you planning on joining your father? Karl asked.

"My dad says Farmington doesn't need two lawyers," Jed told him. Then as others stopped to chat, he shook hands with Karl and wished him well.

Mrs. Carmody appeared at his side, linked her arm through his and led him over to the large picnic table where the lunch boxes were lined up in neat rows, each one numbered. "Let's see who gets the pleasure of our company for lunch?" she said as she took a box and suggested Karl do the same.

Karl examined the number on the box and found himself with a lunch prepared by Amy Glass. Amy happened to be a cute teenager whose mouth fell open when she saw who had her box.

Equally stunned was a young fellow who had the matching number for Mrs. Carmody's lunch.

Mrs. Carmody winked at Karl and led him to where Amy Glass stood and the suggestion that they exchange lunches was greeted with such happy smiles it made Karl feel like a benevolent old man.

"Please call me Winnie," Mrs. Carmody told Karl as she led him to a group of her friends seated at a picnic table, enjoying their lunch. Winnie seemed to know everyone at the fair and as they roamed the grounds, her arm through his, she introduced Karl to everyone they met. "Time you got to know the people you'll be doctoring," she told him.

"College life is teaching me the value of friends," Karl admitted, "but I have a long way to go before I know all the people in Farmington."

"Most everyone knows you," Winnie assured him. "We knew the week you left for college. You weren't out walking."

Karl smiled. It was his walking that was responsible for his day at the fair.

Weary from roaming the fair grounds for hours, Karl went home to sit outside on the bench. It had been an interesting day. Everyone, it seemed, was expecting him back in Farmington to join Doc Hallan. The welcome mat was out, waiting for him.

The opportunities that had tempted him on occasions slowly receded as the warmth that greeted him as he walked among the people of Farmington was all Karl needed to be able to tell himself without reservation, "This is where I'll come as Doctor Vokil! It's home!"

18

The years slipped by and suddenly Karl was home for a short vacation before beginning his internship. After all the excitement of graduation, the quiet of the cottage was a welcome change. Karl unpacked and then went outside to sit on the bench. The patch of yard was as small as ever and the trees hid the sky, but the desolate feeling of those early years away from the farm were forgotten. The cottage was home, just as Farmington was home, and in a few months, he'd be here to stay.

Doctor Vokil. Karl liked the sound of it and wondered how long it would take him to get used to being called Doctor.

From farmer to student to doctor! "There was indeed life beyond the farm," Karl mused with a broad smile.

One year of interning at Rochester General, then back to Farmington. "I'll never practice any place but here." Karl assured Doc Hallan over dinner one evening and they drank to their future partnership.

Marge came early one morning as Karl was enjoying his coffee. Carrying a plate of sweet smelling, freshly baked rolls, she asked, "Am I in time for breakfast?"

Karl took the plate of rolls and still admiring her, happy that she had come.

"Still the loveliest lady in Farmington," he told her.

"My, aren't we chivalrous this morning," Marge declared as she pirouetted. "I think that's only the third compliment you've ever given me. The college girls must have taught you a few winning ways."

Karl smiled at her teasing. "What college girls?" he asked as he poured her a cup of coffee and offered her one of her rolls.

Marge sat, sipping coffee, nibbling on a roll, and her mood became reflective as she forgot the teasing and sat watching Karl. Her eyes softened as she told him, "When you finally made up your mind to go to college, I remember sitting alone, staring out the kitchen window, wondering how the years would change you."

"I thought of the stages you'd gone through, from the silent, brooding farm boy, to the student so eager to learn, and then came the day when you were off to college, your sights set on becoming a doctor."

"There are a lot of things I could say about how, without you, I might still be a brooding farm boy," Karl reminded her, "but I've already given you one compliment today."

"College has made you sassy," Marge scolded, "but it was good for you. Besides becoming a doctor you've learned of a world beyond Farmington."

"And came back," he said.

"For a while, we weren't sure you would."

Karl smiled. "Do you remember the day I spent the day at the fair with Mrs. Carmody?"

When she nodded, Karl told her, "By the end of the day, I knew this was where I belonged. It's strange how quickly indecision can disappear when you're made to feel you belong."

Marge nodded agreement, and told him, "Soon your name will be next to Gary's and after that marriage, I suppose."

"First I have to find the right girl."

"How will you know the right girl when you've avoided girls all these years?" Marge teased, as she always did at the mention of girls.

"I think we should eat the rolls while they're still warm," Karl suggested, not anxious to get back on the subject of girls.

Marge picked up a roll and began to nibble on it, but her mind wasn't on food, and Karl, watching her, said, "Share your thoughts, Marge."

"I was thinking that all the unmarried girls in Farmington will be after you, and I've been wondering if I'd mind losing the special place I've held in your life."

Karl put his arm around her and drawing her close, he told her, "I look forward to marrying and having a family. One more year to go, then back to Farmington for good. It's exciting, Marge, looking ahead to the future. As for the unmarried girls being interested, that remains to be seen." Then, half-jokingly, he asked her, "If I found a special one, you wouldn't mind, would you?"

"I might," she told him without so much as a smile.

Karl laughed at her seriousness. "I do believe you might at that," he said, then quietly reassured her. "Our friendship is important to both of us, Marge. I don't know of anything that can change that. Karl leaned over to give her a friendly kiss on the cheek. Marge turned her head so that their lips met, and Karl, amused at the encounter, was completely unprepared for the pressure of her lips on his, or for his response. He started to pull away, but her kisses held him and as he responded, a surge of excitement raced through his body, arousing in him more than memories. As she pressed her warm body against his, Karl felt his desire heightening. The memories were quickly forgotten, only the moment mattered.

As they lay side by side, still in the languorous aftermath of their lovemaking, Marge's first thought was, "is he going to be shaken by this?" But savoring the nearness of his body next to hers, she chose not to break the spell.

Karl rose on one elbow to look at her and he began to twirl the loose wisps of her hair. "I've always wanted to do that," he said, grinning at her. "The first time I saw you, you were fussing with those wisps."

"I remember," Marge told him, relieved that the nostalgia was still there in his voice.

"I'd never seen a woman like you. You fascinated me. I thought you were dressed for a ball, but there you were, spooning soup into Ma, giving orders, making sure I knew how to boil water. You were always good at giving orders," he teased.

Marge reached out to smack him, but Karl grabbed her hand. "We needed you, Ma and me," he told her. "The Vokil's brought a meaning to my life I didn't know I needed," she told him, a wistful catch in her voice.

"Our relationship has been good for both of us," he told her.

"And this morning?" Marge asked, watching him intently.

Still up on one elbow, looking down at her, Karl told her, "It's what we want it to be, don't you think?

"For me, it's a rare moment of nostalgia when the need to express our feelings needed more than words… a kind of an emotional reaction to the years we've shared, and are over."

The finality of Marge's words surprised Karl.

"There are years ahead when we'll share," he assured her.

"No Karl," she told him. As your life changes, the years of closeness we've had will gradually be no more than a faint memory."

"I find that hard to believe," was all that Karl could think to say as the nostalgia of the early morning vanished.

Marge was suddenly in a hurry to put the morning behind her. She dressed quickly and as she walked toward the door, away from Karl, she told him, "you and Gary will make a great pair of doctors," and Karl heard a touch of sadness in her voice.

Marge's mention of her husband brought a momentary pang of guilt, and watching out the window as she disappeared, their morning together brought not regrets, but rather, a feeling of loneliness, the likes of which he hadn't felt in a long time.

"Something has gone out of my life," Karl told himself as he turned away from the window. We'll be friends but, just as Marge said, the relationship we've had all these years can never be the same. There's nothing left of that young boy that Marge took in hand and liked to tease and boss around. Our lovemaking put a seal on those years. They are part of the past.

Karl's melancholy mood took him outside, but instead of sitting on the bench to brood, he decided to walk, to circle the town, perhaps for the last time.

It had been two years since Karl had traveled the dusty roads of Farmington and he was curious to see the changes people talked about.

Where once it had been an open country, trees had been sacrificed to make room for houses. Except for a couple of bushes standing alone, there was nothing left of the field of bulrushes as the boundaries had been extended and now housed strangers.

"Someday Gary and I will likely know all these people," Karl decided, and as his future came into focus, the loneliness disappeared.

"Our lives will change but Marge and I will always be friends," Karl assured himself, quickening his pace as the exciting thoughts of the years ahead helped push aside the events of the morning.

Back home, Marge went to sit at the kitchen table, her thoughts on Karl and their morning together.

"I sat here the day he decided to be a doctor and thought of the years of college that lay ahead of him and how long it would be before he realized he'd no longer need me. Every time he came home, I waited anxiously, wondering if there'd be a girl on his arm and my heart skipped a beat when he was alone. We were always so glad to see each other, so anxious to share the events of the times when we were apart. This morning, when a single kiss was enough to stir the flames of desire, I couldn't help wonder if he'd been hoping this would happen. I should have known that for him it was just what he said it was, an emotional reaction to nostalgia."

"Karl's thoughts are wrapped up in his future, his and Gary's, one's they've looked forward to and planned for so long."

"Nostalgia!" Marge said aloud, the word sticking in her throat. For her, the morning was beginning to have the taste of ashes.

19

There was still more than a week before Karl was scheduled to report to the hospital and restless, he wondered how to fill the time. His mother and Marcus were always delighted to see him and the walk to their house would be good for him, but their quiet, comfortable lifestyle was not what he needed today. His thoughts kept returning to Marge and their hours together. Thinking about her excited him.

A knock at the door and the sight of Doc Hallan, his heart began to beat wildly.

"How'd you like to spend the day with me?" Doc Hallan asked. "It's going to be a long one. We'll have covered half the county before the sun sets. But it's the middle of the harvest season and people tend to ignore their ailments in favor of getting their crops in. I try to keep my eye on a few of the worst offenders."

Karl went to the kitchen to get his wide brimmed hat, wondering if Doc Hallan's offer had anything to do with Marge, or was it just a coincidence.

Karl followed him out to the buggy and climbed in beside him, still unsettled by his unexpected appearance. They hadn't driven far however, when Karl realized that even if the visit was fortuitous, he was grateful for it, grateful to get his mind away from yesterday.

As they bounced along the ruddy roads and country lanes, Karl got a taste of what the future held and a lesson in the diversity of people and how to treat them.

As Karl had always known, Doc Hallan was a kind and compassionate man, and today he learned that while he was a man of boundless patience, it had its limits.

"Doesn't anyone follow the instructions you give them?" Karl asked when Doc Hallan stopped to check on a new mother.

He found her carrying milk pails from the barn where her husband was milking the cows.

Doc Hallan took the pail from her and gently told her, "It's a bit too soon for you to be carrying anything heavy, Ellie. You go into the house and rest a while with your baby." Then he went to talk to Warren, Ellie's husband.

Doc stood watching while the man went on with his milking. Finally, Doc Hallan raised his voice enough so Warren could hear the doctor's impatience.

"Warren, you know Ellie shouldn't be carrying those pails of milk, not yet. I sent her in to rest. The milk is in the yard. If you expect to have your wife to enjoy in your old age, you better start taking care of her. If you're gonna keep her pregnant you should start thinking about hiring a girl to help out."

Warren looked up from his milking and told the doctor, "I ain't tryin' to keep her that way. It just happens."

"Well, maybe you ought to sleep alone for a while," Doc Hallan suggested.

Warren looked up at him sheepishly and went back to his milking.

"It might seem like I'm sticking my nose into people's private business," Doc Hallan told Karl as they drove along the dusty road to Doc Hallan's next call, "but trying to show people the importance of good, everyday care is a big part of being a country doctor."

"You'll learn a lot this next year while you're interning," Doc Hallan continued, "but you won't get to know many patients, really know them, that is. In the hospital, they come and go too fast. But in a practice like this one you've gotta be there from birth to the grave. It's a demanding, exciting, sad and sometimes discouraging life, Karl."

"If you've got time on your hands the next few days, you're welcome to come with me and get a taste of what lies ahead for you."

Their next stop was to see Mae Tomas. They found her bent over the stove, stirring a kettle of what looked to Karl like applesauce.

Doc Hallan took the big wooden spoon from her and laid it on the table.

"Come sit down, Mae" the doctor said, leading her to a chair.

"But the applesauce," she worried.

"It looks pretty well done," he said. "Now let's take a look at those ankles."

Just as Doc Hallan had suspected, they were swollen so bad he wondered how she could stand. "Have you been taking your medicine?" he asked her.

"I ran out and Jon hasn't had the time to get to town for more.," Mae explained.

Doc Hallan opened his bag and poured a few pills from a bottle. "This'll do you for a couple of days, Mae. I'll remind Jon on my way out to make a trip to town. Now let's see how that heart of yours is doing today," he said as he pulled his stethoscope from his bag and listened to a heart that had been overworked for a long time.

"Why don't you go upstairs and lay down for a while, Mae, give the pills a chance to take hold?" the doctor told her as he helped her up from the chair and led her to the stairs.

"You know all about the harvest time Karl," Doc Hallan told Karl as they climbed back into the buggy.

"These people are as kind as any you'll meet in the years ahead, but their livelihood depends on a good harvest and that means working sun up to sun down. One thing you learn early on is resiliency of the human body," Doc Hallan continued. "It survives, in spite of the abuse we give it. But it still rankles when Jon is too busy to get Mae's pills for her."

The afternoon was well along when Doc Hallan turned the buggy in the direction of Farmington.

"We have one more stop I'd like to make, but it's up to you whether we stop there today.," he told Karl.

"Our farm?" Karl asked.

The doctor nodded.

"Somebody sick there, I gather," Karl said.

"Old man Grange is just barely holding his own. He had a heart attack a while back. His son's taking care of him."

"It's a long time since I've seen the place," Karl told him, "and I wouldn't be much of a doctor if I let my feelings about the farm interfere with helping the sick, would I?"

The Grange's had planted a vineyard where Karl's Pa had planned on putting one, and the pungent smell of grapes welcomed them as they passed the stone entrance that had replaced the wooden gate of the Vokil's. Except for the orchard, there wasn't much to remind Karl that this had once been the Vokil property. The house, the barn, the shed had all been rebuilt or repainted. But it was still there, the feeling for the land tugging at his insides, the memory of his Grandpa just a ways across the field, sitting on the wooden bench under the kitchen window, and his voice reminding him, "there ain't nothin' like the land."

Doc Hallan could see it in Karl's eyes, the pain of remembering. "It's good to be reminded of your roots," he thought as they drove to town in contemplative silence.

It had been a long day and both men were tired and hungry.

"Marge'll have a cold drink and a good dinner ready, Karl, so come join us," the doctor invited him.

Karl wondered how his presence would affect Marge, as well as himself, but her welcome was friendly. Only a wariness in her eyes told him that their lovemaking had caused a feeling of uncertainty between them.

Conversation at dinner revolved around his and Gary's day in the country. Marge sat quiet, saying little.

Later, sitting out on the bench, thinking about his day with Gary, about the patients they'd seen, and the demands on a country doctor, Karl wondered if he'd be up to all that would be expected of him. After a few days with Gary, as he now called him, Karl thought he might learn as much about being a doctor as he would learn in an entire year of interning.

As he walked wearily into the cottage, he felt the heavy sense of responsibility that lay ahead of him, but he'd learned a lot about himself these last few years and had learned to have confidence in himself and his ability and he looked forward to the day when he'd be more than a spectator touring the countryside.

"A lot of patients will be familiar with you when you're finished interning and they know we'll be working together," Gary told Karl on their last tour. "You'll find that a help. People get used to one doctor and often give a skeptical eye to someone they don't know."

"It's been a great experience, and I appreciate your taking me with you," Karl told Gary. "I'll be back before you know it," he said as he climbed down off the buggy.

20

For Karl, the leap from classroom to hospital was just that, a leap. The organized schedule of his college days was only a memory, but the excitement thrilled him.

From the beginning Karl realized Med School hadn't prepared him for the wide range of hospital duties and emergencies, but he came prepared to learn everything they were willing to teach him.

He listened intently as he made the rounds of the patients with the doctors and the nurses, aware of his limited knowledge and hanging on to their every word.

He couldn't help but smile at the unwritten rules that governed interns, the first being, everything is now! And forget the elevator. The stairs are faster. Don't stop to chat and don't expect a lunch break until mid-afternoon.

Always be ready for emergencies, was the warning the young interns had drummed into them as they learned where the equipment was kept and how to use it.

Emergency room duty was always a challenge, as was Karl's first weekend on call. He was the doctor. He was the one who had to make the decisions. There was no room for snap judgments. Weariness carried no weight.

Karl thrived on his life as an intern as acquaintances became friends and a camaraderie developed between him and the staff.

During a lull on the first weekend on call, Karl sat, legs sprawled out in front of him, thinking about the emergencies he'd handled during the past few hours. The call to the cardiac patient on five had been sadly disappointing. He and the nurse had worked feverishly to get the man's heart beating, but he died in spite of their efforts.

But the call to maternity where a young mother was about to give birth to twins made him forget that sad ending.

It was the first time Karl had delivered more than one baby at the same time, and the mother, thrilled as she was, wasn't thrilled more than Karl as he stood in awe at the sight of the newborn babies. He hoped he would always be as thrilled with the miracle of birth.

Karl's few moments of rest were interrupted by a call from three, where a woman was demanding to see a doctor and had half the floor awake with her yelling.

Old and disoriented, needing reassurance, Karl managed to calm her. The nurse was apologetic, but Karl assured her it was all part of the night duty.

When the weekend was over, Karl stood looking in the mirror, grinning with satisfaction at his wrinkled, exhausted reflection and wanted to shout, "I'm a doctor. I'm a doctor!"

Too busy to count the weeks, the final days of Karl's internship arrived with a fanfare he would never have expected.

They surprised him over early morning coffee, doctors he'd worked with, nurses he'd depended on and who had depended on him. There were complimentary expressions of his contribution to the hospital. There were words of appreciation from the doctors he'd worked with, and a gift of a shiny black doctor's bag. Best of all, there was the moment when he was handed his license along with other certificates of achievement.

"There will be other wonderful moments in my life," Karl told his associates, "but I'll remember this as one of the best, the most rewarding and exciting."

Back home in the cottage, Karl unpacked his clothes, sorted through the books he'd want to take to the office, and stood for a moment staring at his new doctor's bag, and his carefully wrapped license. With a smile of satisfaction on his face, he went to sit out on the bench to savor this day.

"To most people, it's nothing but an old weathered piece of wood, a seat held up by four equally weathered wooden legs, but to me it's an old friend that I've shared my life with," Karl mused as he found a comfortable spot.

"Sitting here, as the kaleidoscope of my life slowly come into focus, I'll add a few more pieces to the ever-hanging pattern, this time bright, vibrant pieces of a wonderful year."

21

Karl's step was brisk, almost jaunty as he walked the short distance from the cottage to Gary's office. In one hand he carried his new, black bag and in the other his carefully wrapped license and certificates.

"I'll enjoy finding just the right spot on the wall for these, unpacking my medical books and getting the feel for the office," Karl told himself as he contemplated his first day as a doctor.

Gary greeted him with a firm handshake, a wide welcoming grin, but he had very little time for amenities. "Come along Karl. I'll show you your office where you can put your things for now. You won't mind making a few house calls in the country, will you?" and not waiting for an answer, he told him, "My buggy's outside."

"The Grant baby has croup. He's only a couple of weeks old so we need to keep a close eye on him. Make sure he isn't having a problem breathing, listen to his cough and see that he's getting the cough medicine I left."

"Then stop at Collin's farm. Rory Collins almost cut off his hand with a saw. Check the wound for any sign of infection and put a clean dressing on it. And be sure to tell him to stay away from the barn. On your way back to Farmington, drop this bottle of medicine off to Mrs. Corliss." Gary handed him the bottle. "I told her you'd be along today. When you get back, I have to make a trip to Lockview. You'll have to handle things here this afternoon.

Probably not much doing yet, but now that you're here, we'll start getting busy."

Karl stood dazed, totally unprepared for the onslaught. "Just like weekends at the hospital," he decided.

Almost as an afterthought, Gary told him, "I'm delighted you're here at last. I'll see you at noon."

"Can you give me directions to these places?" Karl asked, pointing to the list Gary had given him.

"I thought you knew the countryside," Gary said, and waving in the direction of the front office, he told Karl, "Ask Annie for directions."

Gary hadn't mentioned there was a third member to their staff and Karl went looking for Annie. "Can you give me directions for these?" he asked, handing her the list, and stood examining her while she wrote down the directions.

"Pretty," he decided. "I like her hair, the color of winter chestnuts. Her skin is so soft looking and fair." It amused Karl how aware he was of fair skin. All he saw in the mirror when he shaved, was the dark, Vokil complexion.

Annie's smile, when she gave him the list of directions, almost made him wish he didn't have to spend his first morning touring the countryside, but when he climbed into the buggy, his black bag on the seat beside him, the list of the sick tucked in his pocket, he knew the thrill of being Dr. Vokil.

"Doctor Vokil, you're on your own at last," he said aloud as he urged the horse to get moving.

Karl studied the list Annie had given him.

A big yellow house on Rook Road, the note said. Sure enough, when Karl turned onto Rock Road, the yellow house came into view.

Mrs. Grant, the baby in her arms, was at the door before Karl was down from the buggy.

"Doc Hallan said you'd be along," she greeted him. "The baby's much better," she told him as she led him into the house and stood watching while Karl examined the baby.

"Doc Hallan'll sure be happy to have you helpin' him. The whole county's too much for one man," Mrs. Grant told him.

Karl was to hear these words repeated dozens of times in the next few weeks.

"How's the baby's cough?" Karl asked. "He's breathing without a problem."

"A lot better," she told him. "The medicine helps."

"One of us will check on him again in a day or two," Karl promised as he was leaving.

Rory Collins was sitting on a tree stump in the yard enjoying the leisure afforded by a wounded hand.

"So, you're the new Doc," Rory greeted Karl and was soon joined by his father.

"Names Jack," he said, putting out his hand to shake Karl's. "Mighty glad to see Doc Hallan's got himself some help."

Karl examined Rory's hand, put a clean bandage on it and gave him the instructions from Gary.

"Stay away from the barn for a few days yet," he advised.

"Won't have no problems there," Jack Collins assured Karl. "Ain't often a farm boy gets to sit around all day."

Karl climbed back in the buggy and examined Annie's direction to the Corliss house.

"It's a long way from the Collin's house, but you're almost back to Farmington when you get there," the note read. In bold letters at the bottom of the page, Annie had written, WELCOME.

Mrs. Corliss greeted Karl with a basket of homemade goodies. "I know you're a bachelor," she told him and thanked him for coming all this way to bring her medicine.

Once in the buggy on the way back to the office, Karl heaved a loud sigh of contentment. He knew there'd be days when he'd be out in the rain and the cold, that he'd meet up with patients sick and grumpy, but today was none of those. It was a day for starting out, a day of warm sunshine, of smiling patients welcoming him, trusting him.

Back at the office, Gary was waiting for him.

"I should be back no later than four-thirty or five," Gary told him as he was on his way out the door, then called back to Karl, "Come have a look." Karl went to join Gary.

They stood together gazing up at their names in bold letters on the newly hung shingle. Gary Hallan, M.D., it read, and under it, Karl Vokil, M.D. They grinned and shook hands. Their partnership was now official.

Gary hurried off, but Karl stood for a moment longer, smiling at the sign that bore his name.

Stepping back into the office, Karl was unsure of what to do next and asked Annie, "Are we expecting any patients this afternoon and what do we do about lunch?"

"You can't be sure about patients. As for lunch, Annie, digging in the drawer and taking out a paper bag, held it up and told Karl, "I'll share it with you."

"I can make a quick trip home." Karl said.

"It's up to you," Annie said with a shrug of indifference, and Karl, remembering the greeting on the note, decided to accept her invitation.

"If you're sure there's enough," he said, pulling a chair up to her desk.

No patients came to interrupt while they ate the cold roast chicken sandwiches or to intrude on the quiet of the afternoon as they were getting acquainted.

"The office isn't always so hectic so early in the morning," Annie told Karl. "I think Dr. Hallan was reacting to your arrival. Until you stepped into the office he was afraid you might change your mind."

Surprised Gary would have any doubts, Karl said to her,

"I'd already told him I was coming back to Farmington to work with him."

"There's a big difference between Farmington and a big city hospital, where you interned. If the offers were good enough, he thought you might change your mind."

"I wasn't tempted," Karl said, a bit miffed with Gary. "I made up my mind quite a while ago that this is where I'd come to practice medicine."

"Oh," Annie said. The conversation lagged.

"Good sandwiches," Karl said.

"Thank you," Annie said.

"Have you lived in Farmington all your life?" Karl asked.

"All my life," she told him. "My father is the county sheriff, has been ever since I was a kid."

"I have a feeling we've met before, Miss Hersey," Karl told her.

"I didn't think you'd remember. Mrs. Carmody introduced us at the summer fair about three years ago. My friend Laura raved about you for days and days."

"Maybe you could introduce her to me," Karl suggested.

"Sorry, Dr. Vokil, but she's married," and Karl could tell by the grin that Annie enjoyed telling him that.

"How long do you think it will be before the office comes to life?" Karl asked.

"People are used to house calls, so it'll take time. Dr. Hallan said he expects more than the usual number of cut fingers to sew up when the farm boys find out they have to come all the way to town, Annie told him, smiling and added, "No matter how tired Dr. Hallan is when he comes back from his calls, he can usually find something to joke about."

"Sounds like the two of you get along pretty well," Karl remarked, then asked her, "You haven't worked here very long, have you?"

"When I got out of school I worked for my father. It was a while before people realized it was a real job, and that I was being paid. After one of the town meetings when salaries were discussed and my name was mentioned for a raise, there was talk that two people from the same family shouldn't be on the payroll of a place as small as Farmington. I would have thumbed my nose at them, but my dad wasn't interested in getting the locals all fired up, so I resigned."

Annie's recitation wasn't without its nuances and sarcasm, but Karl knew better than to get on the subject of the local people. Instead, he said, "And so, Dr. Hallan got a secretary."

"I almost had my bags packed to go to college. I thought I'd start out in business and go from there."

"Go from there?" Karl asked curiously.

"I wasn't sure," Annie admitted, "but I wasn't going to sell ribbons at Mrs. Moore's shop so the townspeople could smirk behind my back."

"Would they do that?" he asked, his tone deliberately denying the possibility.

"Just two or three," she admitted, giving her head a haughty shake.

"And how did you end up here?" Karl asked.

"My father, who else? Doctor Hallan was taking care of my grandmother. He and my dad got talking and next thing I knew, I had a job."

"Strange how things work out, isn't it?" Karl said.

Annie was wiping the crumbs off the desk. "I'm not sure I made the right decision," Annie told him. "Marcie Wells works for Mr. Gargon, the lawyer, and I've often thought if she was to get married or leave the job for some reason, I'd like to work there, see what being a big lawyer is all about and maybe go to college to be one."

When Karl didn't say anything, Annie asked, "What are you thinking? That women don't become lawyers?" There was a trace of defiance in her tone.

"I was thinking that it's not easy for a young lady to succeed in a man's profession," Karl told her.

"That's the general opinion, but I'd like to try. Were there any women in med school?" she asked.

"During my years of studying to be a doctor, there were three women in my class at different times. It seemed to me that they had no choice but to excel, not only to prove they were intellectually capable, but that they would be as able as any man to care for the sick. Someday, because of women like them, it'll be easier for women in what men consider their professions."

Annie stood looking at Karl, surprised at his attitude toward women and asked, "Did those women graduate?"

"Yes, as a mater of fact, they did," Karl told her. "One of them will go into practice with her father."

"How do you think I'd be treated if I went to college to be a lawyer?" Annie asked.

"Quite truthfully, Annie, I'll think you'll do very well right here," Karl told her in mock seriousness.

Annie threw her lunch bag at him. "You're being evasive," she accused him.

Karl ducked the lunch bag and headed for his office.

"I'm going to unpack my books," he told her.

What an interesting day, Karl thought as he started arranging his books on the shelves. "She's an interesting young lady and pretty too. Her grey eyes tell more than she realizes. She's been studying me a lot, but then I've been doing the same with her. Does she know how feminine she is with those long dark lashes and soft pink skin? Am I imagining it or is her smile flirtatious at times?"

Karl suddenly spied the envelope containing his license and certificates. "I can't believe I forgot all about hanging them," he told himself as he went looking for nails and a hammer.

Annie found them and offered to help him. They surveyed the wall carefully before deciding on the right place for his license and his certificates and when they were finally hung, Karl stood back to admire them.

"Take a good look, Dr. Vokil," Annie told him. "It might be a while before you'll have time to admire them again."

It was almost five o'clock when Dr. Hallan got back. He put a folder on Annie's desk and told Karl, "Marge'll have dinner ready by six. If we leave now, we'll have time to relax and enjoy a glass of her homemade wine."

Karl barely had time to say goodbye to Annie and thank her for the lunch, when Gary was out the door. Karl followed and gaped in surprise as Gary climbed into a shiny, black sedan. Sitting imperiously behind the wheel, "Jump in," he invited Karl. "How do you like it?" he asked, smiling from one end of his scraggily mustache to the other.

"It's very impressive." Karl told him. "Quite a step up from a horse and buggy."

"It beats a horse and buggy alright, but it has its limitations. Until we get better roads, it's no good for house calls. Country roads aren't ready for the automobile but it won't be long before the buggy will be a museum piece and all our patients will drive themselves to our office. Won't that be something to see, cars all lined up along Main Street."

Karl smiled at Gary's enthusiasm. "I'm never prepared for these sudden changes," he told him.

"It's not so sudden, Karl," Gary told him. "The automobile has been around for quite a few years. Now it's becoming a reality for the likes of you and me. That guy in Detroit is making sure of that. For your grandchildren, the horse and buggy will be thought of as belonging to the stone age."

Gary drove home, enjoying the smiles and waves that greeted him as he drove along Main Street.

Marge was at the door to greet them, spreading her enthusiasm between the car and Karl's first day at the office.

"How'd it go?" she asked, greeting him like old times.

Karl put his arm through hers, and they climbed the steps together. "My first day as a doctor or my first ride in Gary's new automobile?" he asked.

"Both," she said.

"Both were exhilarating."

"And how did you get along with Annie?" she asked. "Gary says the office can't run without her."

"The office was quiet. Annie shared her lunch with me and helped me hang my license and other certificates. It made me feel important seeing them up there." Karl told her with a wide grin, but when he noticed how intently Marge was watching him, he was glad when Gary changed the subject.

"Wait until you see the shingle hanging outside the office," Gary told his wife. "I was going to wait until Karl got here to help me pick it out, but I got in a hurry to have it hanging outside where everyone going by would notice it and they'd realize I had a partner."

Gary poured the wine and raised his glass. "Here's to a long, happy and prosperous partnership."

Karl raised his glass. "To our days ahead," he said.

Later, when Karl was ready to go home, almost out the door, Gary hollered to him. "Try to get to the office a little earlier tomorrow, Karl. We have a lot to talk about."

Karl grinned and thought of another hectic morning with Gary.

As Karl walked home in the coolness of early spring, he was conscious of the season and its changes. He noticed there were buds on the trees, needing only the sun and early rains to break into leaf. Along Main Street the merchants had their tubs filled with fresh earth, ready to plant the first bright geraniums, and there were window boxes already sprouting daffodils. Karl felt a part of all that was going on around him. His future, like the buds on the trees, was ready to burst forth.

It had been an exciting first day. The ride in the country and getting to know Annie as she shared her lunch. Hanging his license had been exciting because she had been there. They'd laughed at their first attempts to get the nail in just the right place, and when, finally, everything was in place on the wall and they stood admiring it and Karl had looked over to see Annie watching him, and there was an impish grin on her face when her eyes met his.

Karl thought of his evening with the Hallan's, how happy they were to share the events of his first day with him, except for Annie, that is, Karl knew Marge wouldn't want to hear about her.

Once home, Karl had no desire to enter the empty cottage and went instead to sit out on the bench. He wished, as he did so often, that he had a friend with whom he could share the events of the day, along with the school boy excitement of spending the afternoon with Annie, getting to know her as they talked the afternoon away.

During his college days he and Aaron had shared so much that by the time they graduated, they were more than roommates. He'd have enjoyed sharing this day with him. And there was Julia.

"We became friends when I helped her through the labs she hated. She's the first girl I was comfortable with. We studied together, griped together, discussed our hopes for the future, even analyzed our relationship and decided we'd never progress beyond the books and the labs."

Karl missed their easy relationship. She'd have kidded him about what she'd have called his first real crush.

Suddenly Karl remembered his mother. "Both she and Marcus will be wondering about my first day," and ashamed he'd almost forgotten about her. Karl was up from the bench and with the long strides he was known for around town, he headed for their house.

They greeted him warmly and Karl sensed they had been waiting for him.

"We figured you'd have dinner at the Hallan's, but I made your favorite strawberry pie," his mother told him.

In no time, comfortably seated in the parlor, Karl was reliving his day, free to talk about Annie, their lunch together and her helping him hang his license.

"Come and see my office and the shingle hanging outside with Gary's and my named carved in wood," Karl invited them.

"Marcus bought a car" his mother told him. "We'll drive to see your shingle and you can see our car."

When Karl got up to leave, Marcus offered to drive him home. "I'm sure you're tired after a long day and it's quite a walk."

"According to Gary, we'll all be driving cars before long," Karl said as he climbed in the car.

"He's right, "Marcus agreed. "The horse and buggy days are on their way out." Driving Karl home, Marcus told him, "I'm glad you came tonight. With all the excitement I didn't know if you would. Your mother was looking forward to hearing about your first day."

"I enjoyed seeing you both, sharing my day," Karl told him, relieved that he hadn't forgotten them.

At home, getting ready for bed, Karl realized that his visit with his mother and Marcus had been exactly what he'd needed, a chance not only to share the events of the day, but to speak freely about Annie... Annie. "I hardly know her and she's been on my mind all evening. She'll be there when I go to the office in the morning." Karl smiled with anticipation as he climbed into bed.

Karl arrived at the office early, but Gary was there ahead of him, a whirlwind of activity.

"Let's go in my office and put our heads together," Gary suggested.

"I've already talked to Milt Gargon about the partnership," he told Karl as he handed him a legal document. "I'm sure it will cover all the important points of the partnership. You can read it later." Karl took the document.

"You shouldn't have any problems with it," Gary said, as he moved quickly to the next topic. "Now about the schedule," he said as he looked over the sheet on his desk.

"I've mapped out what's fair to both of us. Since you're the new man and need the experience, I've given you three days a week making house calls in the rural areas. People will want to visit a little and get acquainted. It will give you an opening to encourage them to come to the office. I've been trying to get the word out that now there'll be one of us here all the time."

"How does that sound to you?" Gary asked.

"Fine," Karl told him.

"Now there's the matter of getting formally established at the hospitals," Gary continued at the same fast pace. "I've made appointments for later this morning in the Falls, and in Lockview this afternoon. Annie'll have to do her best here alone today. She'll manage," Gary said with confidence.

With the formalities taken care of, and Karl digging in, the weeks began to run together as he covered the county in Gary's buggy.

One morning he asked Annie, "Is everyone in this county sick?" But Karl thrived on the hectic life.

When winter came, long and cold, with mountains of snow piling up everywhere, Karl made house calls in a horse-drawn sled, gliding over the unplowed roads, stopping at homes where the kitchens were steamy hot and the smell of freshly baked bread filled the air, inside and out. There was homemade soup, thick with vegetables and meat, that the women insisted on sharing with him, giving him jars to take home, kidding him about his singleness, his need for a wife.

No one was more aware of this need than Karl. The cottage had never seemed so empty and when he dwelt on the loneliness of his life, his thoughts turned to Annie. From that first day at the office when Annie shared her lunch with him and helped him hang his license, Karl had known there was something special about her.

It wasn't long before he realized that his turn in the office were the best days of the week because she was there.

He found excuses to go to her desk just to look at her and see her smile, and at the end of the day when he returned to the empty cottage, he knew the loneliness would be with him until she became his wife. He was in love!

As she dropped a message on his desk one morning, Annie pointed to the window and told Karl, "It's snowing again, just when we thought we'd seen the end of it."

Karl looked out at the snow coming down and at Annie and thought what fun it would be to take her on a sleigh ride.

"You're serious, aren't you," Annie said, laughing when he suggested it. Her face lit up with surprise and pleasure when she realized he was serious.

The sleigh ride was their first date on a day so cold Karl had covered the horses with thick blankets and felt the thrill of Annie's closeness as she snuggled under the big fur rug.

They traveled across the county all the way to Lockview where they found a café that served creamy hot chocolate.

Annie tried to make snowballs, but the snow the was dry and fine, not good for snowballs. But she threw a handful of the dry stuff at Karl as she climbed back into the sleigh and laughed at him as he wiped it off his face. He laughed with her and bent and kissed her and her smile told him she liked it, so he kissed her again and this day was the beginning of their courtship.

Over numerous dinners at the Hershey's, Karl got to know Annie's parents. With Annie's friend Laura and her husband, they explored Niagara Falls. They took the train to Buffalo to dinner and a movie. They spent evenings with Karl's mother and Marcus, and there were evenings when happy to be alone together, they walked hand-in-hand along Main Street.

"Now its time to ask Annie to marry me," Karl told himself one evening. "We've courted long enough."

Karl plodded through the rain to the office, his mind on Annie and his decision to ask her to be his wife. But the rain hadn't kept the patients away and he's had a busy morning, with hardly a moment to think about her. Now, with the last of the patients gone, Karl stood at the window watching the rain. He planned on taking her out to lunch, and over lunch, asking her to marry him. But, not in this weather.

Karl turned to see Annie standing at the door of his office, brown bag in hand. She pointed to the rain splashing against the window, waved the bag and asked, "Care to share?"

"Are you sure there's enough?" Karl asked with a big grin as he cleared his desk. "Didn't I share your lunch once before?" he asked, his brow furrowed as though he was trying to remember.

"It was an exciting day for you, your first day as a doctor," Annie reminded him.

"And the first time I met you," he said. "I thought about you the rest of the day and all evening. I tried to remember the exact color of your eyes and how you tilted your head when you laughed, and I've thought of you every day since then."

Karl moved his chair close enough to Annie to kiss her, and when he said "I love you Annie. Will you marry me?" She was momentarily speechless, her eyes wide with surprise that quickly turned to happiness. "You know I will," she told him without a moment's hesitation.

When he kissed her again, it wasn't the gentle caress that Annie was used to. "Oh Karl," she exclaimed, pushing him away. "You've never kissed me like that before."

Karl laughed at her and Annie laughed too. The sandwiches were forgotten and Annie let him kiss her again, and they'd sit smiling at each other and then Karl would kiss her again. "I've wanted to ask you to marry me for a long time," he told her.

"You surprised me today," she said. "You could have asked me a long time ago. Why didn't you?" she asked him.

"I'm not sure Annie," he said. "I think I wanted to give us both some time to be sure."

"I knew the first time you kissed me I'd say yes if you asked me." She told him with a toss of her head.

"That day on the sleigh ride, our first date?" Karl said in disbelief. "It was the coldest day of the year and you couldn't make a snowball because the snow was too fine to pack, so you threw some in my face. You would have said yes, way back then?" he asked.

"You remember that day!" Annie said surprised.

"I remember it very well," he told her. Kissing you was the best part of the sleigh ride," and as he held her close, Annie told him, "I think I started to fall in love with you the day I shared my lunch and helped you hang your license."

"Perhaps we both fell in love a little that day," Karl told her.

22

The Hershey's were delighted but hardly surprised when Karl and Annie told them the news, but Mrs. Hershey was aghast when Annie suggested a date in June for the wedding.

Gary was equally delighted, but hardly surprised. He's watched the progress of their relationship from the day he noticed how often the two of them went back and forth to each other's office.

Gary invited them to dinner and apologized when he had no champagne to celebrate the announcement.

"Prohibition takes half the fun out of life," he told them.

"Fortunately, Marge makes great wine," he said as he reached in the buffet for a bottle.

Marge shared the announcement with a handshake for Karl and a hug for Annie, but her warm, easy manner was missing.

Alice Dole, when Karl told her the news, felt that life was now complete for her son. Karl's marriage to Annie would bury, once and for all, the sadness of their early years.

23

Sitting on the bench one evening after he and Annie had announced their plans, Karl was thinking of the happiness their marriage was bringing to those he loved.

Except Marge.

"Things have changed between us, but we both knew they would. I've been busy, and when I go there, Gary and I seem to do all the talking. After the years when she directed my life, when we shared so much, she feels left out and my marriage is taking me one step further away from her. I had hoped she'd be truly happy, knowing I'd no longer be lonely."

Karl, so familiar with loneliness, knew that without him, Marge was very much alone, but he couldn't turn back the clock to those years when he depended almost entirely on her. He couldn't believe she wanted him to.

Karl vacillated between showing Annie the cottage or looking for a house. It's going to seem pretty small after her parent's spacious house, he realized, and yet he was reluctant to give up the cottage. When he showed it to her, she surprised him by telling him, "It's just right until we need more room."

Annie's wedding preparations were crowding everything out of her life, "even me,' Karl complained as she pushed him out the door with no more than a hurried kiss.

"I can't look forward to seeing you at the office since you no longer work there, and evenings when I come, I'm not sure it's worth the bother of taking off my coat."

"Oh, Karl, don't be so grumpy," Annie kidded him. "Our wedding is only a week away."

Karl was up with the sun on his wedding day and pulling on his trousers, he went outdoors to examine the sky. Over to the east were a few bright splashes of color as the sun crept over the horizon and Karl smiled as he thought how happy Annie would be to have the sun shining on her wedding day.

Digging in his pocket for a handkerchief, Karl wiped the dew off the bench and sat down to enjoy the early morning quiet. He was sure that as the hour of his wedding drew closer, he would, like all bridegrooms, be nervous and excited, but right now, as a wave of happiness coursed through his body, Karl buried his head in his hands and his heart overflowing with thanksgiving, he prayed that every day he shared with Annie would bring happiness to them both.

Marcus came to drive Karl to the church and then, waiting for Gary, Karl stood alone in a quiet corner and watched as the church filled to overflowing, amused as he heard the wistful voices, excited over the romantic wedding of the young doctor marrying the sheriff's daughter.

Karl spied Gary coming in a side door just as the church bell sounded the arrival of Sheriff Hersey with his daughter.

With an apologetic smile that turned to a mischievous grin, Gary joined his friend, Annie's brother.

They waited as Jim and Marcus escorted the last of the guests to their seats, then with a nod to Karl and Gary, the two started up the aisle.

There was a sudden hush and then a whispering of excitement as the strains of the wedding march filled the church and heads turned to catch a glimpse of the bride as she stood for a moment before starting up the aisle.

Smiling, Annie took her father's arm and with her eyes fastened on Karl, she walked slowly up the aisle, beautiful in a gown that shimmered in its whiteness, her dark hair and face covered with a veil that didn't hide the smile on her lovely face.

Karl's outstretched hand was waiting for his bride as she took the last couple of steps, and then the pastor was talking, first to those sharing this day with the bride and groom, and then to them, Karl and Annie, as he led them through their vows.

The hush that had filled the church during the vows now echoed with good wishes as Karl and Annie walked down the aisle, their eyes aglow with happiness, sharing the moment with their friends.

The young, unmarried girls were lined up outside the church, hoping to catch the bride's bouquet, and as it soared through the air and was caught by a pretty young girl, more hearts than hers were filled with dreams.

With old shoes and tin cans clanking behind their new car and rice falling off them with their every move, the newlyweds waved goodbye and were gone.

Marcus had offered Karl his fishing cottage. "It's rustic, but comfortable, so long as you know how to light a fire, and the lake is beautiful," he told them. And now, oblivious to the world beyond the cabin, Karl and Annie spent their days in undisturbed bliss.

To the back of the cabin was a wooded area, in front, the lake. They sat on the shore and dangled their feet in the cold water. They hiked through the woods long enough to get tired, then went back to the cabin and fell into each other's arms. For one whole week, theirs was a world inhabited by just two people.

24

Annie was awash in the joys of marriage. She loved her husband, loved the freedom of not having to go to work every day, loved cooking Karl's favorite food. She had only one complaint. Her husband refused to teach her to drive.

"I don't think ladies belong behind the wheel of a car," Karl told Annie. Annie disagreed and only the newness of their marriage kept her from arguing with him.

For Karl, coming home at the end of each day, was, as his grandfather would have said, pure bliss. The wooden bench sat unused, as life with Annie left no room for his old habit of bench sitting. And yet, at times, the urge was there, and he went out one evening to sit alone and think about life, its sudden changes often abrupt and cruel, and then, as if to apologize for its heartlessness, it showered you with such happiness you could only bow your head in grateful acknowledgment.

Pregnant with her first child, Annie was overjoyed, as was her husband. She remade the small bedroom into a nursery. She sewed and knitted and filled the baby's chest with not only her own layette, but with the steady flow of gifts from both grandmothers-to-be.

As the months of her pregnancy dragged on, Anne turned her bedroom mirror to the wall so she could endure her bulky body without having to look at it.

Karl's endearments, his patience, his half-hearted attempts to assure her that she looked fine did nothing to ease her discomfort.

When she gave birth to a son and the excitement of the family swirled all around her, Annie wanted only to be left alone with her wounded body. Not even her own mother had prepared her for such an ordeal. She was especially upset with her husband. "You're a doctor," Annie had moaned as her labor dragged on. "You never told me how bad it would be."

They named the baby Alex Joseph, after Karl's brother and grandfather, and with the help of both grandmothers, Annie survived to share in the joys of her first child.

The christening party, held at the Hershey home where there was room for friends and relatives to gather, was indeed a happy occasion, the first real get together since the wedding.

Karl noticed Marge, from a quiet corner and taking her a glass of punch, he went to sit with her.

"Not as good as your wine," he told her as he handed her the glass.

"You don't come to share my wine very often since you got married," Marge complained.

"Nor your homemade cookies," Karl joked, intent on keeping the conversation light. He reached for her hand.

"Come join the celebration," he invited.

"After I finish my punch," she said, but it wasn't long before she was saying her goodbyes. Karl walked her to the door, determined not to make apologies for his busy life.

"Stop by the cottage, Marge," he invited her. "Annie would be delighted to see you."

"I'll stop one day soon," she said, and not waiting for Gary, she left to walk home alone.

"Why is Marge so aloof, so cold toward us and the baby?" Annie asked her husband as they drove home from the party.

"Perhaps it's a feeling that comes from watching everyone make a fuss over the baby when you've never had children," Karl said without conviction, aware that her coolness went back to his courtship with Annie.

His attempts to bring her into a friendly relationship with the family had failed and Karl could only wonder if his marrying had brought an end to their friendship. Next to Annie and his grandfather, Karl had never felt closer to anyone, but now, it seemed to Karl, she was deliberately shutting him out.

"Marge, Marge, why are you shutting us out?" Karl wanted to ask her, but he knew he'd be wasting his time.

25

Marge's inclusion into the Vokil household came about just as it had in the beginning, because of an act of mercy.

The town and surrounding countryside were laid low with a virulent flu epidemic that left few families untouched.

Gary came home, barely able to stand after a day of caring for the sick of Farmington. As he covered the town and its outlying areas in his car, Karl traveled into the countryside in the buggy, handing out cough medicine, aspirin and advice as the bug seemed not to want to let go. "Karl's worried," Gary told his wife. "The baby's cough is worse and Annie, up all night, is hardly able to stand. They both have a fever. I stopped at the Hershey's, but they're still struggling to take care of themselves. Annie needs help Marge," her husband told her, not aware of the coolness she had developed toward Karl.

"I'll go, of course," Marge told him and heard his sigh of relief.

Marge went with a freshly made kettle of soup. She began by sponging the baby in hopes of getting his fever under control, then she spooned a little warm broth into his mouth, drop by drop. When he coughed, she managed to get a few drops of medicine into him and after he dozed a bit, she started the entire procedure over again, until at last he fell asleep in her arms. When he woke, it wasn't with a cranky cry of a sick child and Marge knew the fever was under control.

Annie slept fitfully, taking aspirin for her fever and sipping the soup that Marge kept on the table next to her bed.

"The baby?" she kept asking every time she woke up.

"He's a lot better," Marge assured her, and relieved, Annie crawled back into bed and slept until her fever left her and she could struggle out to the kitchen to eat a healthy bowl of Marge's soup.

Marge stayed to help with the baby until Annie was well enough to get along on her own. During the days of Annie's convalescence, they sat together in the small parlor, gazing out at the bare trees, wishing the sun would shine, and slowly became friends. Once again, Marge's kettle of soup, her act of mercy had opened a door, one she had closed.

One evening, Karl sat watching as his son walked the entire length of the living room and into his father's open arms. "When did he get all that confidence?" Karl asked his wife.

"He's a very determined child," Annie told him. "He took a few steps and decided, no more crawling. Falls didn't discourage him. He got up and tried again. He's very proud of himself."

When Alex had worn himself out showing off, Annie put him to bed and came back to sit next to her husband.

"Karl," she told him, "it's time to look for a house."

Karl put his arms around his wife and pulled her close. "Of course," he told her. No explanation was necessary.

It was Marge who told them about the Shuman house.

"Gary's been taking care of Art Shuman's yearly onset of bronchitis," Marge told Annie. "Art's determined to move south before winter sets in, this time permanently."

They went together, Annie, Karl and Marge to see the house. Annie stood in the front yard examining it.

"When you don't like it from the outside, it never really welcomes you," Annie told them.

"And what have you decided?" Karl asked after she had stood for several minutes, head cocked one way and then the other.

"I was hoping I would have a large, front veranda, but I think there's a porch on the back," then still examining it, she told them, "the house has a look of stability about it. Brick houses always do, and the casement windows give it character, don't you think?" Annie asked both Marge and her husband, and not waiting for an answer, she climbed the steps and rang the doorbell.

"Inspect the house at your leisure," Mrs. Shuman told them, opening the door wide for them to come in. "Mr. Shuman and I are on our way out."

Annie moved slowly, examining the house a little at a time. She started at the beautiful staircase, with its dark mahogany banister and boldly carpeted stairs. It was hard to imagine the living room without the expensive Shuman furniture and thick carpets, but Annie was thrilled with its size.

"And look at the beautiful fireplace, Karl," Annie said. "We haven't had a fire since our honeymoon at Marcus's cottage." Annie went to examine the dining room and the kitchen and then raced up the stairs.

"Come on up, you two," she hollered from the top of the stairs. "Four bedrooms with big closets," she told them, "and the wallpaper looks like it was put up yesterday. Isn't it lovely," Annie exclaimed. "The whole house is so bright and airy, but it doesn't look like anyone lives in it."

"That's because their children are grown and have moved away." Marge told her.

"We'll take care of the empty bedrooms," Karl said, standing in the doorway, grinning at the expression his remark brought to his wife's face.

"What do you think, Karl? Should we buy it?" Annie asked.

"I'd buy it for the yard alone," he told her. "All the windows look out on a well-kept yard and there are tall maples shading a path that almost circles the house. On the one side of the path there are rose bushes, some still in bloom, and you can see the sky... It's a wonderful place to raise a family."

Annie wondered if he'd looked at the inside of the house at all and followed him down stairs, taking his hand as she led him through each of the rooms.

Karl agreed the house was lovely and took them outside to examine the yard. The smell of the rich earth, the breeze rustling the trees, the open sky. Karl felt closer to the land than he had since leaving the farm. And there on the side of the house facing the roses, Karl saw just the spot for his bench. He put his arms around his wife and they stood admiring what would be their home for many years.

Moving day was like a celebration, or so it seemed to Karl. The women, Annie, her mother, Marge and Alice Dole were all there, unpacking as quickly as the boxes were brought in. Preparations had been going on for weeks. Fabrics had been chosen, curtains sewed and hung. Family members offered pieces of furniture, some of it that had been tucked away in attics for years. They polished it until it shone like new and placed it in just the right spot so that the house needed only a family gathering to add the final touch.

When the last load was on the cart, and the cottage was already losing its personality, Karl walked alone through the empty rooms, unprepared for the emotional impact of leaving. He soaked up the memories. A whole lifetime had been lived here. It was here he finally found solace from the tragedies of the farm. It was here, with the help of the Hallan's, a new life opened up for him, and it was here he had brought his bride and his first child. It was here he had found real happiness.

"A lot of memories." It was Marge's voice.

"Yes," Karl agreed. "A lot of memories. Their eyes met and held, a moment of intimacy passed between them, and Karl, linking his arm through hers, walked her out of the cottage. Later, Karl went back alone to retrieve the bench.

26

Karl and Annie christened their second son, Linus Andrew, after Annie's grandfather, who was the first of their family to come to America.

There was another child for the Vokils. To Annie's delight, a daughter they named Emma. And almost five years later, when Annie, complacently settled in the routine of a young matron whose childbearing days are over, found she was pregnant again.

"Oh Karl," she moaned. "Life has been so wonderful just the way it is. And now I'm going to have another baby to spoil everything."

"Annie, Annie, how can another baby spoil your life? You'll be just as happy with this one as with the others," he insisted in his reassuring doctor's voice. And he was right.

The baby, when she was born was so different from the others with her shiny bald head and eyes as blue as the violets in her mother's kitchen window, that Annie forgot she hadn't wanted this baby.

"I've decided to call the baby Lucy," Annie told her husband. "I want her to have a name all her own, not after Aunt so-and-so or cousin so-in-so."

This baby that was going to spoil her life, is special to her, Karl realized and told her, "Lucy is a very pretty name."

Just as Karl had predicted when they first examined the red, brick house, the four bedrooms were taken care of and the house was alive with a growing family.

Alex, a true Vokil in appearance, was big and dark like his

father and at times Alice wondered if he didn't have a little of his
father's melancholy nature. He liked to play ball with his friends in
the big open field behind the house. But once he learned to read,
Annie often found him in a quiet corner where he could be alone
with a book.

Linus was everything that drove a mother crazy. He was determined not to be taught, bounding through the house as well as
outdoors like a young, unfettered forest creature. At times, he was
the bane of his older brother, but his sister, especially Lucy, adored
him. He taught Emma how to slide down the banister without
falling off when she reached the end, and he piggy-backed Lucy,
because she was too little to slide down alone. He took them in
the woods back of the house and showed where there was a pool
of water where they could sometimes find s frog. He fed the dog
when it sneaked under the table at mealtimes, and had a way of
talking his father out of a spanking when his mother insisted he
needed disciplining.

Unless Linus was around to tease her and get her giggling,
Emma was a quiet child, content to play with her dolls. Once she
learned to read, like her older brother, she liked to be left alone
with a book, although her mother was never sure if she wasn't often
hiding from her sister and her demands "to come play with me."

Lucy was all the things her mother dreamed she would be. The
bald head was now a mass of golden curls, and the blue eyes had lost
none of their vibrant color. As the baby of the family, she learned
how easy it was to get her own way.

For Karl, these were years of happiness. His heart overflowed
with love for Annie and their children. Evenings when he sat out
on the bench, it was to read the daily paper, or when one of the
children climbed up to sit with him, he'd tell them stories about his
grandpa and his years on the farm. And as Karl Vokil was sharing
the past with his children, the world was changing, and even the
small town of Farmington was moving forward.

27

The "Roaring Twenties" with its tales of speakeasies, bobbed hair, short skirts and fast dancing girls was slow to intrude on their lives. But the day did come when husbands came home to find their wives shorn of their braids and neatly coiled buns, and watched in disbelief as hems climbed to expose legs that had been hidden for hundreds of years.

The Prohibition Act of 1922 introduced an era of bootlegging that thrived wherever there was a source of liquor that could be smuggled in and the Niagara Frontier was no exception.

But it was in the big cities that bootlegging introduced a new era of corruption that would affect a large part of the country. Murder, political patronage, or 'graft' as it came to be known, grew by leaps and bounds. Greed, it seemed, had taken on new dimensions.

Dr. Karl Vokil was too busy to concern himself with Prohibition or its impact on the world beyond Farmington. His concern was for his partner.

"There's something bothering Gary," Karl told Annie as he stood in the kitchen watching her prepare dinner rather than sitting out on the bench as he usually did. "I've never known him to be so quiet."

"Have you tried to talk to him?" Annie asked her husband.

"There's an aloofness about him that keeps you at arm's length," he told her. "In all the years we've been together, I've never known Gary to act so strange."

Annie stopped what she was doing and looking directly at her husband, she asked him, "Have you noticed Marge hasn't been around lately?"

"No, I haven't noticed," Karl had to admit.

"She's left Gary," Annie told him, and Karl, completely taken by surprise, was quick to disagree with her.

"That's ridiculous, Annie. Marge would never leave Gary. Where did you ever hear a story like that?"

Annie chose to ignore Karl's obvious disbelief and as calmly as she could, she told him.

"It's another woman, a nurse from the hospital in Lockview." When Annie added, "she's pregnant," Karl's angry voice startled her. "Who told you that?" he asked, his dark eyes glaring.

Annie wasn't surprised at his anger or his unwillingness to give credence to what she was telling him, but difficult as it was, she answered him. "My mother told me, Karl, and it's been going on for a long time."

Annie hated what she knew this was going to do to his and Gary's relationship.

"And you didn't tell me?" he asked, indignant that she's kept something so important from him.

"I wasn't sure how you'd react if I told you.," Annie explained, "Working with him every day… I was afraid…" her voice trailed off.

Karl's anger, simmering near the surface, was about to explode when suddenly, he thought of Marge. "Marge! Where is she? How long has Marge been gone?" Karl asked, frightened as the terrible implications of her absence hit him.

"I don't know how long she's been gone, Karl. A week, maybe longer. Marge hasn't been stopping like she used to," Annie told him. "I wasn't worried, just curious," she admitted, then told him all she knew of the sad tale.

"Marge has known for a long time that Gary was seeing another woman," and went on to explain.

"It was when I was getting over the flu. We were sitting in the living room and Alex was asleep in her arms. Marge talked about the early years of their marriage, how happy they were, how the bell was always ringing in the middle of the night, someone needing a doctor. She told me about her friends and how much fun they had together until they started having babies. And almost in a whisper, she told me about going to a doctor and having him tell her she'd never have children."

"It was late afternoon," Annie continued. "We weren't much more than shadows in early winter darkness. I knew she was crying and I didn't know what to say. I remember reaching for her hand but not saying anything. And after a bit, she told me how not being able to have children had affected their marriage and she knew Gary had a woman in Lockview."

Annie finished with tears running down her cheeks.

"You've known all this and never said a word. Why Annie?" Karl asked, confused and deeply disturbed.

Annie looked imploringly at her husband, "Karl, I always thought Marge hadn't meant to tell me as much as she did. She minded about the nurse in Lockview but I know divorce never entered her mind."

"Divorce!" Karl was stunned.

Annie nodded yes.

"How could Gary do this to Marge?" Karl shouted.

"Karl, you'll frighten the children," Annie warned, and told him, "Gary has probably put himself in a position where he may not have a choice but to divorce Marge."

Karl thought about this possibility and agreed with Annie. "That would explain a lot," he said, but this latest piece of news increased his fears for Marge.

"Karl, the children are making an awful racket. I'm sure they're starved. We can talk later," Annie said and went back to making dinner.

"I'm not sure I want dinner," he said, and went outside. The bench beckoned him as it always did, when Karl needed to be alone with his thoughts.

Stunned about the two people he loved dearly. Karl sat, his head buried in his hands, questions, one after the other, beating against his brain, his thoughts on Marge and the years of their friendship.

Marge never mentioned children. In fact, she never gave any indication of any problems.

Shocked with this realization, Karl was forced to examine their relationship more closely.

"I was always wrapped up with my own life, the past as well as the future, welcoming Marge's help, her friendship, only vaguely aware that she needed my friendship."

"Why did I never wonder why Marge wanted me to make love to her that morning long ago?" he asked himself. As he continued to analyze bits and pieces of their relationship through the years, he wondered why he hadn't been more aware of the lonely side of her life, why his visits had been so important to her and why his marriage almost ended their friendship permanently.

"But, what if I had known there were problems in her marriage? What if she hadn't hidden the dark side of her life? What could I have done?" And Karl knew instantly it was better that he hadn't known.

"Oh God, Marge," Karl moaned aloud, "where are you? Your being alone frightens me and it saddens me that that you couldn't come to us instead of disappearing. But you couldn't, could you, Marge? You shared your secret with Annie once, but not this time. There is bitterness as well as pain now."

28

At the office the next morning, Karl stood watching Gary as he was busy going through some files. As he stood looking at him, he saw the man he had always seen every day these past twelve years, a man of average height, neither fat nor thin, wearing thick lenses that hid the color of his eyes, with a mustache that always needed a bit of trimming, and as particular as ever about his dress.

"But he's not the man I thought I knew," Karl realized. "There's so much we never know about each other, so much deliberately hidden even from those closest to us."

Karl went about the few house-calls he'd agreed to make, his mind still on Gary.

"Doc Hallan," Karl had called him when he'd first known him. "He'd come when his Pa died and helped his mother bear her grief. He'd come regularly when they hadn't known if she'd survive the miscarriage." Remembering the days he'd spent with Gary as they traversed the countryside during the harvest season, keeping an eye on patients too busy to take care of themselves, Karl knew Gary was still the caring man he was then. "Whatever the problems in his and Marge's marriage, I will not judge or belittle myself by doing so," Karl told himself decisively.

Friendship as firmly rooted as ours should have no limits, even at the worst of times. Returning to the office from his calls, Karl heard Gary call to him. "Come in when you have a minute."

Gary dropped his bag on the floor and went in.

"I suppose you've heard by now that Marge and I are getting a divorce," Gary told him in a flat, unemotional tone.

"Annie mentioned it," Karl said, his tone noncommittal.

"Well, I didn't ask you in here to discuss my private life," Gary told Karl, not even looking at him. "My concern is our practice and how to work things out. I already know your feelings about Lockview. Too bad. We'd have done well there."

When Karl said nothing, Gary continued. "Asking patients to come all the way to Lockview is pretty much out of the question. It seems to me the best solution is for you to buy my share of the practice."

"Are you telling me you're going to set up a practice in Lockview alone?" Karl asked, doing his best to hide the shock of Gary's decision.

"That's what I have in mind," Gary told him, his tone flat, making discussion impossible. It had been a long time since Karl had been confronted by such a hopeless situation. It was more than just the breakup of their practice that concerned him. It was the breakup of a friendship that he had considered rock solid. The divorce would mean losing them both. The finality in Gary's voice told him that their friendship was not a consideration.

For the next few days, waiting for Gary to give Karl some indication of his plans, and hoping to hear from Marge, Karl wore Annie down as he talked about nothing else.

Finally, she told him, "Karl, when you have some news, tell me, for now, let's talking about something else."

As the days passed with no word from Marge, Karl could stand Gary's silence no longer, and asked him, "Is Marge alright? Nobody has heard from her?"

Gary stopped what he was doing, raised his head to answer Karl, and told him, "Not a word, I've not heard anything." Karl heard the fear I his voice. When He asked him, "Can I do anything?"

"Pray," Gary told Karl. Karl left Gary's office, every inch of his body trembling.

Two days later, Gary received word that Marge had been found in her car in a town he'd never heard of, an empty bottle of pills in her lap.

The shock left Karl numb.

Annie wept uncontrollably when Karl told her the news of Marge's death, but was able to put aside her grief and go about her job of taking care of her family. But when Karl sat out on the bench hour after hour, her anger flared.

"Is that how you deal with sorrow?" she asked, "sitting alone on the bench."

Stung, Karl could only stare at his wife, and Annie, seeing the hurt expression on his face, regretted her outburst, and went back in the house.

Karl sat thinking about what Annie had said. It was true he did handle heartbreak differently, did find solace sitting alone on the bench. But the bench wasn't to relieve sadness only. "How can I explain to Annie about the bench?" he asked himself.

"My earliest memories are of my Grandpa pulling me up to sit beside him. I sat alone on the bench to mourn when he died, but not just to mourn. There were so many memories and I wanted to remember all of them."

"When Grandma left to live with Aunt Hilda, I took the bench home. My brother Alex and I sat out on it that night before he left, and I sat there to mourn when the war took him. Later, I sat remembering the years we spent together."

"Someday, Annie, when they are older, our children will remember that we sat out on the bench together, and just as Grandpa told me, I'll tell them stories about a life they'd never know unless I told them. It's their only link to the past. There is a need to know that you are more than a fleeting second in time, that you are a link in a chain that goes far back even as it goes forward."

"I can go out, and sitting on the bench, I relive so much. The happiness, the sorrow, the dreams, the love I feel for those close to me. What would you think, Annie, if you knew how, when I'm sitting alone, I remember our happy hours together, and how I like it when, in the cool of the evening, you come to sit with me. And now I want to sit out here and think about Marge, about the sadness in her life that she hid from me. And about all the good things she did for me and Ma, and how empty my life would have been without her. Sometimes, like now, Annie, I like to sit quietly, alone on my bench."

29

Gary returned from Marge's funeral, subdued and uncommunicative. Karl waited for him to make the first move, but he went on seeing patients, occasionally going out on emergency house calls, saying as little as possible.

"How can you stand working with him?" Annie asked Karl regularly.

"Leave it be," Karl told her and knew from the way she flounced out of the room that his remark displeased her. When she came back to join him, Karl told her, "He's suffering Annie."

"He deserves to suffer," she told him coldly, which was the exact reply Karl expected.

It was over a year before Annie saw Gary gain. Karl was at the hospital, delivering a baby, and Lucy had fallen out of her wagon onto the gravel walk and blood poured from both knees. Annie wiped them and iced them but there was no stopping the bleeding or Lucy's screams. Against her will, she took her to have Gary check to see if the one gash needed a stitch.

Annie was appalled when she saw him. He was suddenly an old man, more white than brown in his hair, and the mustache, scraggily as always, was pure white. But it was the gauntness of him that struck Annie's heart, and his quietness as he took care of Lucy's knee.

"Would you like to come to dinner, Gary?" Annie heard herself ask him.

The doctor gave her a wistful smile. "Thank you my dear, I would indeed like to come to dinner," he told her and Annie was sure she saw a tear trickle own his cheek.

Karl came home to a table covered with a fancy table cloth and Annie's good dishes. "We're having company, I see," he remarked to his wife.

"Yes," she told him. "Gary's coming to dinner."

Karl walked over and put his arm around his wife.

"He's so sad looking, Karl, I couldn't help myself," she explained.

"Don't apologize, Annie, it's one of the nicest things you've ever done."

Without the children the evening might have been a disaster, but they were quick to recognize him and greet him and make him feel welcome as only children can. But he was not the Gary Annie remembered.

"Is he as quiet at the office?" Annie asked her husband after Gary had left. "He's so different from the Gary we knew."

"He's lost his lightheartedness, but with the patients he's still the caring man he's always been," Karl told her.

"And you to him?" she asked.

"We aren't as comfortable with each other as we used to be. We don't share the laughs and frustrations that lighted up a busy day," Karl told her, then added, "he needs our friendship Annie, so I hope you'll ask him again."

"Bring him home anytime," Annie told her husband. "The children will put a smile on his lips."

Gary came often. He raised his eyebrows when the children called him Grandpa, not at all prepared for such a title, but they all had a good laugh about it.

"Gary's more like his old self," Annie told her husband. "The children are helping him forget."

"Not forget, Annie, deal with it," he wanted to tell her. Instead he said, "Gary enjoys being part of the family."

It was the end of the day, the patients had been cared for and sent on their way, and the two doctors were tidying up their offices. "You coming to dinner?" Karl called to Gary.

"Do you think Annie and the children could manage without you tonight?" Gary asked. "I though the two of us could go to the hotel for dinner.

The deliberate casualness of Gary' suggestion told Karl that Gary had more on his mind than dinner.

"Sure," Karl agreed. "I still remember the first steak I ever had at the hotel."

"I was busy introducing you to the life of a country doctor," Gary told him. "A long time ago," Gary added with a touch of sadness.

At the hotel, Gary chose a table away from the other diners and Karl knew he had been right. Gary had something on his mind.

As they sat sipping a glass of wine, waiting for their dinners, Gary told Karl the reason for their quiet dinner.

"I'm leaving Farmington," he told Karl. He could have been talking about the weather, so casual was his announcement. Karl felt as if he'd been hit by a rock.

Gary, choosing to ignore Karl's stunned expression, continued, "I'm not going to dig into the past, Karl, other than to tell you that I could never convince Marge that disappointment is not rejection, and that I loved her very much."

"We all loved her, Gary," Karl told him.

There was nothing casual about Gary's next announcement.

"Karl, I have a son," he told Karl. The pride was restrained, but it was there. "He lives in Albany with his mother. His name is Mark and he'll be three years old next month. I've decided to remarry and be there to celebrate that birthday with them."

It was quite a speech and Gary, having delivered his news, sat back, studying Karl, sipping his wine, waiting for him to absorb the impact the news would have on both their lives.

Karl surprised Gary by reaching across the table, hand out-stretched, and told him, "It's a decision you'll never regret, Gary."

It was an emotional moment for both men and Gary, shaking the proffered hand, told Karl, "I didn't know what your reaction would be."

"Only happiness for you, Gary." Karl assured him.

"It wasn't a hasty decision, Karl," Gary told him.

"Farmington has been home to me for a long time and you and I have been good friends as well as associates. I'm leaving you with a heavy load, Karl," Gary admitted without a sign of guilt. "But I've spread the word the word at three hospitals and in the next issue of the journal. If Mark's birthday wasn't so close, I'd have stayed until we had a replacement, but it was suddenly important that I be there."

Karl smiled. "Annie reminds me every day for a week to be sure not to make any late appointments when one of the children has a birthday. As for the office, someone will come along. Walking into an established practice should be a pretty good inducement, wouldn't you say?"

"It's the rural bit that scares them," Gary said, but you're right, the inducement is there."

Annie was waiting up for Karl, curious, but not prepared for the news her husband brought home.

"It's strange, Karl, but I've noticed a change in Gary lately." Annie said. "Foolishly, I attributed it to his association with our boys."

"It probably impressed on him what he was missing," Karl told her. "When he said he had a son, you should have seen him Annie. He was so proud. I've never seen him so excited."

"Did he mention Marge?" Annie asked.

"He wanted me to know he's always loved her."

Annie nodded. "I always knew he did, but it wasn't enough, was it, for either of them?"

"I suppose you're right," Karl agreed. "But I was glad Gary chose not to dwell on Marge's death. When he said Marge took disappointment for rejection, I couldn't help but think that Gary's disappointment when Marge told him they'd never have children may have been greater than he admitted, even to himself. Marge saw his reaction and she never forgave herself, never," Karl said sadly.

"But watching Gary tonight, so proud, eager to get away... I'm going to miss him, more than I realize. But he's going to enjoy raising his son," Karl said with an enthusiasm that had Annie wondering if he'd still feel the same after a few weeks of carrying on alone.

Once the realization that Gary was leaving took hold, Annie planned a farewell dinner, inviting a few friends and doctors he'd worked with at the hospitals through the years.

And then he was gone, leaving the people of Farmington stunned. A moving van emptied the house and a local realtor was given the job of selling it.

Karl struggled with the problems of running the office alone, unable to believe Gary wouldn't walk in the door one morning as he'd done for so many years.

It was a few months before Gary's word about the opportunity in Farmington reached an interested doctor.

His name was Roger Castairs, young and eager as Karl had been to hang his license on the wall and get down to the business of taking care of the sick in Farmington.

Connie, the receptionist, took him on a tour of the town, introduced him to the local merchants and the town pharmacist. Annie invited him to dinner.

"Just think, Karl, you'll have a day off in the middle of the week again," Annie reminded her husband.

30

For the Vokil family, one year passed into the next, as the children grew and began to take on lives of their own. Annie made sure she kept her husband abreast of their changing lives.

"Alex made the football team," Annie told Karl. He was so excited he forgot his books, and had to go all the way back to get them.

"Linus needs some pressure put on him to get his marks up. His report card is on the buffet," Annie told her husband.

"I'll talk to him," Karl promised.

"Please be firm with him," Annie insisted. "He needs more than your usual kind approach."

Karl smiled as he reached for the report card.

"Have you noticed how pretty Emma is getting now that her permanent teeth are all in? She thinks she's too tall for a girl. To cheer her up, we went shopping for new dresses. I think that helped her feel better about her height."

"Karl, there's a very important football game this Saturday, and Alex wants me to remind you that you promised you'd be there."

"When do I forget football games?" Karl asked, and assured her, "I hadn't forgotten. Annie, you didn't tell me he'd made starting quarterback."

"I knew he wanted to tell you himself. How did you find out?"

"He stopped at the office on his way home from school."

"I hope you made a fuss over it. It's the biggest thing in his life right now."

"Annie, my love, don't I always encourage the children?" Karl asked, pretending to be offended.

Amused, Annie told him, "I'm never sure what you're telling them when they're out on the bench with you."

"I promised Lucy I'd be at the ballet recital next Friday," Karl told Annie as they were getting ready for bed.

"It starts at seven so we'll have an early supper. "You'll be able to get home on time, won't you?" Annie asked. Can't Roger handle these late appointments?"

"Probably," he said. "I'll mention it to him."

Crawling into bed next to her husband, Annie told him, "The years are flying by so fast Karl. Lucy in school, Alex in high school. Can you believe it?"

"The years haven't changed the way I feel about you," Karl told Annie as he pulled her close and felt the thrill of her warm body next to his. "Let's forget the children for now."

31

The stock market crash of 1929 that resounded throughout the business world made the barest of rumbles in Farmington but the Great Depression spared few families throughout the country as the nation changed from a land of confident, hard-working, cheerful people to vast areas that knew want, poverty and despair.

President Roosevelt instituted work projects and a form of relief to help the country's desperately poor, and in time the depression began to ease. But its demise was followed by greater fears than poverty as a new enemy emerged. By the time his name was on everyone's tongue, Hitler's goose-stepping troops had conquered one country after another and the world was in the throes of what cane to be known as World War II.

The horrors of the steady bombing of London alerted Americans to a world of devastation never before dreamed possible.

There was no lack of sympathy for countries Hitler marched through with his well-trained armies, or for the bombed-out city that had endured the nightly onslaught of Stukas, but there was hope that America could stay out of the war and that American youth could be spared.

Peal Harbor changed all that. Outraged by the attack, America set her sights on defeating its enemies and this determination resulted in America becoming the arsenal that supplied the world, not only with guns, tanks and bombs, but with manpower.

The draft law was enacted. Throughout the country, recruiting stations were hastily established and long lines of young Americans eagerly lined up, were signed up, trained, outfitted and sent off to fight in countries that up to now, had existed only on maps.

Karl Vokil was deeply troubled. The war would demand of him his two sons.

Alex, the older of the two boys, was finishing his senior year and making plans for college. His draft notice would quickly follow his eighteenth birthday. And indeed, it did, right on the heels of his high school graduation.

It seemed to Alex's parents that their son had barely received his draft notice when he completed his training at boot camp and was home for a short visit before being shipped overseas.

"I feel like I'm on a fast-moving train with no stops," Annie told her husband when Alex came home for his final visit, "speeding along into a world that's being thrust on us before we've had time to learn where it's taking us."

They sat together at the dinner table, the Vokil family and Bonnie, Alex's girlfriend, listening to Alex's stories about boot camp, trying to pretend it was just dinner as usual.

Karl found himself studying his son intently. Knowing he would soon be gone, it was as though he needed to memorize his every feature. "He certainly carries the Vokil genes," Karl had to admit. "In fact, we both look like my grandfather Josuf, the thick, black hair, the black eyes, tall, well built."

It's no wonder Alex was the star of the football team. He towered over the other players. He's always been a determined young fellow. What he wanted he went after, but never like a bull in a ring. Karl, remembering Alex running down the football field, defying anyone to take the ball away from him. Karl had to smile. "There is a little of the bull in him, at that," he decided. "He'll need it where he's going."

Karl turned his attention to Bonnie, Alex's girlfriend. For years he thought of Bonnie as Emma's girlfriend and then one day he realized it was Alex and Bonnie.

"What will the years do to them?" he wondered. "Give them a chance to grow up, to see if the love they have for each other will weather the years they'll be apart. Alex won't come home the same person he is now."

Karl turned his eyes back to his son, and overwhelmed with love for Alex, his first born, he felt them grow misty.

"I'll get the coffee," he said, and Annie, watching her husband and sharing his fears, let him go for the coffee, something she could not remember him ever having done before.

A few days later, Karl, his family and Bonnie stood on the station platform saying goodbye to Alex. Karl and Annie had driven them to the station, and Alex, his arms tight around Bonnie, whispered to her of his love. "I'll be back," he promised.

They stood quietly while the train pulled out, waving as Alex passed them. Bonnie continued to stare until the train was no more than a black spot in the distance.

Emma went over and led her to the car. "Come home with is, Bonnie. We'll shed a few tears over coffee."

Even though they had been friends all their lives, neighbors growing up on the same street in and out of each other's houses, Bonnie could not share her feelings with Emma. The conversation was forced, desultory, as Bonnie waited for what was a decent time before leaving.

"We'll share any news with you," Emma promised as she walked her friend to the door.

Once at home, Bonnie went to her room to be alone and to think. "A few months ago, who could have thought it possible that we would be standing at train stations, waving goodbye to our schoolmates, one after the other, and the day would come when it would be one of the dearest to us who would be boarding a train, off to war."

Stretched out on her bed, Bonnie lay thinking of that goodbye, and their promises to each other. She could still feel the warmth of their last tight embrace, the sadness in their last kiss, a memory that had to last, "how long?" she wondered.

Bonnie lay thinking of their last weeks together, how they'd allowed the excitement of graduation to push aside the grim pictures of war, knowing that soon, that war was going to change their future.

With Alex's draft card coming so soon after graduation, the war was there, on their doorsteps, taking charge of their lives. For how long?

No matter what the radios blare, no matter how horrible the newsreels, Bonnie would never think of her future without Alex, never. She would make life bearable, begin preparing now, for the first time when he would be home.

Bonnie's, mother called her for dinner, and as they sat enjoying her mother's apple pie, Bonnie told her parents, "I've decided to be a nurse."

They nodded in approval.

Dinner at the Vokil household that evening was subdued. As Emma and her mother cleared the table and washed the dishes, Karl went out to sit alone on the bench. Alex's empty place at dinner upset him. "Will I ever breathe freely again?" he wondered as he swallowed long gulps of air to ease the tightness in his chest.

"How long? How long?" Karl asked himself each day as he read the reports in the newspaper and listened to the latest news on the radio. "The news is bad. The war continues to escalate with new enemies entering the conflict and no clear victories."

"And Linus. He too will have to go," Karl told himself, not at all heartened by the fact that it would not be for a while yet.

Annie came out to warn her husband that the evening chill would give him pneumonia.

"Will you sit with me, Annie?" he asked his wife.

"Things never seem so bad when you're near." His hand reached out for hers and he smiled as she carefully examined the bench before sitting on it.

32

They came one at a time, to say good bye.

"Soon they'll all be gone, Karl said as he shook hands each of their son's boyhood friends and wished them a safe return.

Annie hadn't given much thought to Emma and the young lad who came calling, other than he was very good looking, well-mannered and had a car. At sixteen, it seemed normal that Emma would be dating.

When Emma told her mother, "Paul will be the next one leaving," Annie stood back and looked questionably at her daughter. There was a catch in her voice that did not belong to a sixteen year -old.

"He's eighteen and expects his draft notice any day," Emma continued, ignoring the knit brows and startled look in her mother's eyes. "We're kind of engaged," she finished with just a touch of cockiness.

There had always been an independence about Emma that at times Annie admired, and at others annoyed her.

"I will not get into an argument with her about this," Annie told herself. "The war is hastening relationships that will change between now and the time they come home." So, she only said, "He seems like a nice young man."

It was only a matter of days before Paul came with his draft notice waving it as though it was the American flag and he was the proud standard bearer.

Emma grabbed him and hugged him and the next thing Annie knew, they were hanging on each other, making promises of eternal, undying love. Annie went out to the kitchen, not sure whether to laugh or cry. "They're so young, trying to grow up too fast, pledging undying love because they think that's what it's all about. The radio plays romantic ballads, the movies make farewell such sweet sorrow. How many promises made in the madness of the times, will be broken.?" Annie asked herself. "How much sadness lies ahead?"

It seemed there was no end to the good-byes. Ed Thorton came by. Ed was the high-school quarterback when Alex first made the team and Alex always said it was because of Ed's interest in him that he had developed his ability to become the team's starting quarterback.

"Your brother will be next," Annie said, "and then all our boys will be gone."

"Will didn't pass the physical," Ed told her.

Annie stared at Ed. "Why?" she asked. "Will always seemed as healthy as you and the rest of the boys."

"Something to do with a valve that doesn't always close. Too much stress or pressure can cause serious problems with the heart," Ed told her. "Dr. Vokil can explain it to you better than I can."

When Will stopped by later, his rejection was evident.

"I feel like a cast-off," he told the Vokils. "This valve problem is nothing new. Doc Hallan told my mom about it when I was a kid. It's always been one of those 'don't worry about it' things that suddenly turns into a major affliction." Will's dejection deepened as he continued his tale.

"You simply can't imagine the feeling of worthlessness that comes over you when there you are, standing in line with a hundred other guys, naked as the day you were born, and the guy ahead of you who barely reaches your shoulder gets the okay, and the Doc listens for a minute to whatever it is goes on inside you and says, 'sorry son,' hands you a paper, and without more than a glance, calls out 'next,' and you're left standing there, dazed as well as naked and the gruff voice tells you, 'move along, keep moving.'"

"What did your parents say?" Annie asked, trying to hide her amusement at Will's recounting of his harrowing experience.

"My mom knew more about this valve than she ever let on and wasn't surprised when I was rejected," Will told them.

"Why is going off to war so important to you Will?" Karl asked him.

The question surprised Will. He sat looking at Karl, not quite sure how to answer him, and told him as sharply as he dared, "Basically, right now, all we want to do is get even with those Kamikaze pilots who bombed Peal Harbor and would like to wipe us off the face of the map. There's anger and revenge burning inside everyone I know, young and old, and the older one's expect us young guys to do what has to be done."

"It's a pretty normal reaction, don't you think?" he asked, looking from Annie to her husband.

"I'm sure it is," Karl agreed, aware that he angered Will, but he chose to let the matter drop, and as Annie walked him to the door, he called out, "Be sure to keep in touch, Will."

Annie walked back to the couch. "Do you feel reprimanded?" she asked her husband.

"If that's what he intended, then I suppose I do," Karl answered, "but I think in his disappointment, he chose to take offense at a rather simple inquiry. I admire every lad who goes off to do his part. But it doesn't make me feel any less American because I can't stand the thought of how many of our boys won't be coming back to us."

"You worry too much Karl," Annie told him.

"I suppose I do," he agreed, then asked her, "Would you like to go for a walk with me? Maybe to Thorton's for ice cream, take our minds off Will and his reprimand."

Annie smiled. "It's better than sitting on the bench," she told herself as she went for a sweater.

With graduation only a few weeks away, Linus stopped one day to see his father. Karl saw the red car drive up in front of the office and smiled as he watched his son jump over, rather than open a door.

The car had belonged to a friend who had been drafted and Linus begged his father to buy it for him.

His mother disapproved. "He's barely passing, Karl. Give him a car and he may not even graduate," she warned and later told her husband, "He's nothing but a playboy. Every time the car goes by, all you see is girls, girls, girls. And have you heard the horn he bought? It frightens the birds out of the trees and every dog in the neighborhood starts to howl," she told him indignantly.

But Karl, always aware of what the future held for his son, was reluctant to curb his spirits. "He's young, Annie," he told his wife. "Let the boy enjoy himself."

Now, Karl stood, watching his son as he walked toward him. "Do you know why they put doors on cars?" Karl asked him.

Linus was amused that his father had seen him. "It's quicker that way," he joked as he went to sit in a chair facing his father's desk.

Karl, realizing his son had not come for gas money, as he often did, went to sit at his desk. The seriousness of Linus' face prepared him for what he was sure must be on his mind.

"Dad, there's something I want to tell you," and though hesitant at first, Linus didn't stop until he finished what he'd come to say.

"Rather than be drafted, I've decided to signup for the Army Air Force. I'd like to be a pilot and if I wait until I'm drafted I'll probably end up in the army carrying out the garbage or some such equally edifying job. I might as well choose what I want to do."

Doing his best to hide his feelings, Karl reminded his son, "You haven't graduated yet."

"Dad, graduation is less than a month away, and I'll be eighteen in two months. We both know I'll have to go. I'd rather do it my way," Linus told his father with a determination that belied his easygoing manner.

When Alex had been drafted and gone overseas, Karl had told himself, "there was no need to worry about Linus. The war would surely be over by the time he was eighteen. But now, two years later, the war was still raging, and here is Linus, a few months away from his eighteenth birthday, telling me he wants to be a pilot. My God, a Pilot! Those German's and Japs have been shooting them down like flies."

Karl got up from his chair and moved to stare out the window. The sight of the red convertible unnerved him even more. It seemed to personify his son. "Not much Vokil in him," Karl mused. "Between Annie and my mother, both he and Lucy have inherited a different set of genes, different personalities. Fun, laughter and a zest for life have been added to the more serious Vokil personality."

Linus went to stand next to his father. "Dad, I'm sorry," he said, and Karl felt his concern.

"You knew I'd be upset, didn't you?" his father asked.

Linus nodded.

"It's not just your decision to be a pilot, son. It's this whole mess. Who'd ever thought the war would go on and on, that it would spread like a conflagration that we seem not to be able to contain."

Karl turned to his son, "Thank you for telling me, here alone in the office, where, if I make a fool of myself, only the two of us will know."

Linus put his arm across his father's shoulder in a gesture of understanding then quietly left the office.

Karl turned back to the window and watched as Linus climbed over the door and sped off in the red car as though he didn't have a care in the world.

Asking Connie, the receptionist, to reschedule his appointments, Karl left the office. He went to tell Annie about Linus when the two of them were alone in the house.

The news brought a loud wailing from Annie that surprised Karl. He hadn't realized how much the war was wearing her down.

"What if we had three sons or four sons? Would they take them all?" she asked her husband, sobbing and angry.

Karl put his arm around her and held her while she cried on his shoulder, then, wiping her eyes, she went to sit in her rocking chair.

"You have your bench. I've learned that my rocking chair was meant for more than putting babies to sleep," she said as she began to rock gently.

Karl smiled at her reasoning.

"The house will be quiet with Linus gone," he said.

"Yes," she agreed, and added, "He's very special to you, isn't he?"

Surprised at the question, Karl was not sure how to answer. "He certainly makes life interesting," was what he finally said, aware that it wasn't a very satisfactory answer.

Later, when Annie and the girls were in the kitchen helping their mother, Karl went out on the bench to think about Annie's remark that Linus was special to him.

It was true. He had always been so. But Karl could not mentally flog himself because his second son brought him a kind of joy that was different form the other children. It had little to do with his love for them.

Love. The most talked about and the least understood of all mankind's qualities. Love is not something that can be doled out, a teaspoonful here, a cupful there, according to the date of a child's birth, the qualities that please you or the traits that annoy you. Karl knew he loved each one of his children in a way that complemented them for the very way they were.

"Who can explain the special kinship that exists between two people?" Karl asked himself. "Why did I fall in love with Annie almost from the day we met and never feel an ounce of love for any other girl? Why do I have the utmost admiration for Alex, but it is Linus that brings a smile to my lips, the faster beat to my heart? And why does the thought of him as a pilot frighten me so?"

It was Lucy who shook him free from his worries as she planted a kiss on his cheek and told him dinner was on the table.

When Linus came home for dinner that evening, his mother hugged him a little harder and held him a moment longer and he knew his father had told her of his decision.

When Linus told his sisters of his plans, Lucy's startled, "Oh no!" as she stared at her brother, sent Annie hustling to the kitchen to hide her tears. When she came back carrying a plate of rolls, Lucy was quizzing Linus about the red car, her tone light, but Annie noticed that she held her fork so tight it was a wonder it didn't snap in two.

"I'm afraid you're a bit young for a car, Sis," Linus told her. "Emma is next in line," and turning to Emma, "it's all yours," he told her.

"Would you mind if I had it painted a less conspicuous color?" Emma asked.

"There's a certain notoriety about owning a bright, red convertible," Linus told her, "and you just might enjoy it."

Between them, Linus and Lucy kept the dinner conversation lively, Linus acting as though nothing in his life changed, and Lucy, doing her best to pretend she believed it.

Later, when Annie and Karl were getting ready for bed, Karl remarked to his wife, "There's a special closeness between Lucy and Linus, isn't there?"

"It's been that way since Lucy was able to climb on his lap and get whatever it was she wanted," Annie told him. "Linus has always been a friend to her. There a bit alike, don't you think?" she asked, and Karl, sitting on the edge of the bed to remove his socks, sat holding one, thinking about what Annie had said.

"More than I realized," he admitted. "They understand each other."

As he climbed into bed, he told his wife, "Lucy would have enjoyed the red car."

33

Of course, Linus was accepted in the Army Air Force.

"They didn't even have to wait for the ink to dry before they assigned him to training school," his mother complained, "and they chose one as far away as possible."

"They sent him to where the weather is better for flying," Karl explained, but Annie refused to be appeased.

"Annie, Annie," Karl said consolingly. "Don't be so angry. Come, we'll go sit out on the bench for a little while. It's such a lovely day. Have you noticed how the roses are ready to burst into beautiful color?" Annie reached for his hand. "Yes, I've noticed," she said and went to sit next to him on the bench.

A few days later, Karl came home with the news that Roger had joined the medical corps and would be leaving at the end of the week.

"Every day something new to deal with," Annie grumbled. "With no one to share your load, how will you manage?" she asked him.

"I might as well give you the rest of the bad news," he said. "Connie is leaving to work in one of the war plants. I'll soon be running a one-man office."

"I'll gladly give up my volunteering at the hospital and come to work for you," Annie offered.

"Well, perhaps I'll have to accept your offer, Annie," and then with an imploring look, he asked her, "do you think you could come tomorrow? I didn't tell you that Connie been gone for almost two weeks."

Annie stood staring at her husband. "I think I'm still on the fast-moving train, Karl, and still waiting for it to stop so I can get off."

"I didn't expect everyone to desert me, at least not both of them at the same time," Karl's tone was contrite but desperate. "You're sure you won't mind working for me?"

"This has turned into a strange world, a world we could never have imagined. But we'll manage," she said with as much optimism as she could muster. "I'll be at the office in the morning," she promised.

Karl went over and kissed his wife. "Thank you, Annie," he said softly.

Annie went to work the next morning just as she'd promised Karl she would, and was amazed at how different things were from the days when she worked for Gary. There were few lulls in the day as patients filled the waiting room and the telephone rang incessantly. "How long is Karl going to be able to manage alone?" Annie asked herself as one hectic day followed the next.

The waiting room buzzed with conversation that reflected the times as patients discussed coupons and ration books, and of course, the shortage of gas. They laughed at the Friday fish day of Catholics. "Who doesn't eat meat on Friday's, and sometimes the rest of the week as well?" they joked as they tried to make light of the shortages. But as the war dragged on and they struggled to keep a smile on their faces, they couldn't always hide the worry and fear that was as much a part of their everyday lives as coupons ad ration books.

When Emma graduated from High School, she took over her mother's job at the office.

Annie couldn't believe how nice it was to be back at the hospital emptying bed pans, rubbing backs and running errands, jobs she thought she hated. The day to day atmosphere of a doctor's office had worn her down so that at the end of the day she was as weary as her husband.

There was little real news in the letters from the boys, mostly the confirmation that they were well, missed the family and sent their love. Will Thornton came with the news that his brother Ed had made captain and there was no hiding the fact that he still resented being left behind. "I might as well go to college as hang around and mope," he'd told the Vokil's on one off his visits.

Will's visits home from college always included a visit to the Vokil's, when as Lucy liked to remind her family, he talked about something besides war.

One evening as Will sat at the Vokil's discussing the changes going on all around them, Karl asked Will, "How do you like the latest style for women?"

"Women wearing pants?" Will said laughing. "I had this conversation with my mother earlier today and she almost blasted me out of the house when I told her pants were for men."

"Wait and see," Karl warned Will. "When the war is over and women are no longer climbing around in the airplane factories, they'll still be wearing pants."

"Think so?" he asked incredulously.

"Look how quickly women bobbed their hair and shortened their skirts," Karl reminded him. "When was the last time you saw a woman in a long skirt doing her shopping?"

Lucy came bouncing down the stairs. "I'd buy a pair of pants, but mom won't let me," she complained.

"And hide those lovely legs," Will joked.

Lucy giggled. "You think I have nice legs?" she asked Will, pulling up her skirt to expose a little more.

Karl, watching this exchange, shook his head. "Annie's right when she reminds me that the world is changing," he told them.

As the war dragged on, the shortages, the rationing, these

excuses were no longer of major concern. They had been replaced by fear and loneliness. The patriotic speeches had been given and forgotten. Patriotic songs no longer quickened the step. The news-reels tried to keep morale high with clips of bravery and heroism, but alongside these were graphic pictures of those whose bravery had cost them their life. Rumors began to circulate of young wives and girlfriends frequenting bars and nightclubs, drinking too much and not too particular about the company they kept.

The Vokil family did its best to keep life moving in a normal fashion in spite of the times and their fears.

Lucy made fun of her sister as she made a beeline to check the mail the minute she was home from work, looking for a letter from Paul, but Emma wasn't any different from her parents as they waited for word from their sons.

Occasionally, when Will was home for a few days, he took the girls to the movies. "Our big date." Lucy liked to joke as she complained about the absence of guys her age.

Lucy was fast losing her schoolgirl looks as she grew into the beautiful girl her mother was sure she would, the day she saw the shiny head and blue eyes. But, for Lucy, looks didn't mean a whole lot when there was no one to admire her.

At home one evening, the house was too quiet even after a tiring day, Annie asked her husband, "Where have the years gone? It seems only yesterday that the only way we had peace was to put the children to bed."

"Those were the good days," was her husband's only answer. Annie worried about him. His quietness disturbed her. "He seems so far away from me at times. It's more than the long hours caring for the sick. What is he thinking?" she wondered. "Is he on the battlefield with Alex or in a plane with Linus?" And Karl, whose married life had been so free of tragedy, was aware how quickly things could change, that tragedy lurked around the nearest corner.

"Don't be such a worrier," Annie chided him often, but as the war dragged on, she shared his fears.

When the telegram was delivered, Annie was home alone. She recognized it for what it was, but she did not open it. Instead, she called her husband and asked him to come home. Her hands shook when she handed him the envelope.

Sorry to inform you...

Linus's plane had been shot down.

As a doctor, Karl had heard the cries of many women, but he had never heard the plaintive cry like the likes of Annie's. He tried to hold her close as she wept uncontrollably but she pulled away from him and went to her bedroom. He followed her and sat next to her on the bed, gently rubbing her back, as sobs racked her body. There were no words of consolation, only the sharing of their loss. When, exhausted from crying, Annie dozed. Karl went to sit alone on the bench, and head bowed, he too wept.

As neighbors, friends, and even strangers offered their condolences and shared their sorrow and told of their own losses, Karl and Annie realized that pain was all around them. The list of casualties read like a litany.

"When will it end?" was the question on everyone's mind.

It did end.

34

Church bells rang throughout the country. In small towns like Farmington, people gathered on Main Street, rejoicing. There was hugging and kissing and tears. In the cities the celebrations were wild and endless, with ticker-tape falling like snow in the streets of New York. But when the hoopla was all over, the broken hearts were not mended, and the crippled were not whole again.

The boys started to come home. Small groups first and then boatloads and planeloads.

From the day they said goodbye four years ago, Bonnie had thought of nothing but Alex's homecoming. She had graduated from nursing school, worked at the City Hospital where she had taken her training. She found a small apartment that was within walking distance of the hospital, and saved her gas coupons for emergencies and the day when Alex would come home. She saved every penny so she'd be able to help him with his college tuition.

And they would marry.

Alex's last letter came a week ago.

"No one is telling us anything," he wrote, "but we sense the war is winding down. New rumors are flying around us every day and for the first time we believe there is substance to them. Soon we may be able to pick up our lives where we left off a long, long time ago. Bonnie, Bonnie, I love you."

Bonnie spent the following weeks in a frenzy of preparation.

First, she cleaned the apartment until it shone. Then she started on herself. She creamed and tweezed and examined her face carefully.

"Have I aged?" she asked herself as she stared in the mirror. "My hair, is it too short? Alex never liked short hair. And do the freckles on my nose still stand out? Will he tease me about them?" Bonnie wondered.

"Oh, Alex, let everything be alright between us," she prayed and then, as she always had, she pushed aside the thought that years could change anything between them.

And then, one day, the news came that he was on his way home.

They stood on the platform, Bonnie and Alex's family, watching the train slowly chug to a stop. Instantly a mass of khaki clad bodies poured out, eyes searching for familiar faces. Bonnie watched as Karl Vokil spotted his son while he had one foot on the train step. She watched the reunion between father and son, between mother and son, the careful scrutiny as they examined each other from head to toe, the hugs and quiet words of welcome as they tried without success to hold back the tears.

Then the two girls, Emma and Lucy, grabbed his neck, and were kissing him.

"How straight he holds himself," Bonnie thought. "His hair isn't clipped nearly as short as I thought it would be. How broad his shoulders are."

Looking over the heads of his family, Alex glanced in her direction and when he saw her, without ever taking his eyes off her, he walked toward her. Bonnie reached for his hands and held them in her own.

She looked into his face. It was the same face she had known and loved, but there were lines that stretched down along his cheeks that hadn't been there before. But the eyes that were looking into hers were as large and dark as ever and glowed with happiness and love. Alex pulled her to him and held her close, repeating her name again and again. Feeling the strong arms around her, she felt safe. The fears, the fits of panic were gone, forever.

For Alex, the homecoming was wonderful and unbearable. The unceasing attention of his family made him uncomfortable, and the quiet was unnatural.

On the battlefield there was no such thing as silence. Occasionally, if there was a short lull, there might be time enough to look around you, to check to see which of your buddies was still there next to you, to scream in anger at what you saw, and then as the bullets began to fly around you and with the sound of guns so near, you vented your anger, spewed out a few expletives and kept moving.

When you weren't on the battlefield there was always the need for distraction, the need to shut out the quiet that allowed time to think about the horrors you had witnessed, been part of. In the mess hall, in the barracks, wherever men gathered, the talk was loud, crusty man-talk, punctuated with roars of laughter, and the sound of heavy boot pounding the wooden floor. Only sleep brought a measure of silence. And now, in this strange quiet of peace, Alex missed his buddies and the noise they generated.

35

"It's time I examine the town," Alex told his mother after he'd eaten the breakfast she'd fixed him and sat with her until they'd emptied the coffee pot.

"Not many changes, Alex, but it's still a pretty town," she told him.

"Thanks for fixing breakfast, Mom," he said and kissed her lightly on the cheek. "It's good to be home."

Alex knew the remark didn't express what either of them felt, but words didn't come easy, not yet, and the need to keep moving was still strong in him.

"We aren't at ease with each other yet," Annie told herself as she watched her son go out the gate and turn towards the town. "And we haven't mentioned Linus."

As she turned away from the window and went to clear away the breakfast dishes, her thoughts turned to Alex and Bonnie and their need for more time together, the chance to get to know each other again and make plans.

"I never gave a thought to all the adjustments there'd be, for all of us, but especially for Alex," Annie told herself. "I thought having him home was all that mattered."

Annie worried that the pleasure of homecoming was being replaced with anxiety, her own. "Alex needs time to work his way back into our lives and I need to see his restlessness for what it is."

With strides long and deliberate, much like his father's, Alex walked into town and along Main Street. He was surprised at how easily he recognized faces, how good the welcome felt as hands reached out for his. "Welcome home, welcome home," they repeated, one after the other.

"I'm really home," Alex told himself when Ian Thornton laughing, invited him into the drug store, for an ice cream cone. "Alex Vokil, Alex Vokil! My God. It's good to see you," Thornton repeated as he led him into the store.

"Come back where we can sit for a while and talk," Thornton said as he led Alex behind the counter where there were a couple of stools.

"I suppose you've heard that Ed is Major Thornton and intends to make a career of the army," he told Alex. "And Will graduated from college and will soon take his CPA exams. He plans on having his own accounting business someday." Then he laughed. "He's still complaining about what the army did to him."

Alex listened, as Thornton talked on, bringing him up to date on everything that had happened in Farmington since Alex had left, intent on telling him every little detail. When he started giving Alex names of the boys who weren't coming home, Alex knew it was time to leave.

Alex spent an evening with a couple of old friends, fresh from the battle, as he was. They met at a local bar, marveled at the good taste of American beer, talked about the old days before the war when they were too young to go to bars, exchanged feelings about how great it was to be home with their families and girlfriends. When the silences began to grow longer as each one seemed to retreat deep in his own thoughts and memories, they finished their drinks and said good night.

Alex walked home slowly, thinking about Bonnie and how little time they'd shared since he came home.

Careful not to intrude on what she felt was Alex's need to spend his first week home with his family, Bonnie had not pushed herself into their reunion. She came each day after work, spent the evening with him and his family, but with each passing day their need to be alone with each other became intolerable.

Bonnie came early one day, and as casually as possible, she told the Vokil's, "I've managed to get a few days off work and I've come to whisk your son away for a few days."

Alex rushed up the stairs, packed a small bag, said goodbye to his family and was gone, climbing into Bonnie's car while his parents still stood at the open door.

The drove a few miles in silence, glancing at each other often, savoring the feeling of being alone at last.

"Do you know how long I've dreamed of just you and me, alone, getting to know each other again, having fun, making love?" Alex hesitated, then added wistfully, "We never have, you know."

Bonnie couldn't help but laugh. "Do I know we've never made love? Yes, I know, Alex," she said with a longing that matched his.

At her apartment, Bonnie took Alex's bag and led him into a small living room. "Make yourself comfortable," she told him, "while I put on a cup of coffee."

"No coffee, thanks," Alex said as he followed her, and when she turned, there he was, arm reaching out for her, and alone at last, he held her, kissed her long and tenderly, then passionately. The long years apart were forgotten.

The next few days were wonderful and strange, wonderful because they were together, because there was no rhythm to the days, no sense of time passing.

From the first night together, Bonnie discerned that Alex had ghosts to bury, memories to agonize over, and she made no demands on him. She listened when he talked, sat quiet when he was quiet, fed him beer and hamburgers with mustard and relish and onion and tomato, walked miles with him, and when his dark eyes softened and held hers, her body came alive as they reached for each other.

Bonnie awoke one morning to see Alex standing, curtains pulled back, staring out the window.

"Did I tell you about being in London with Linus?" he asked her, his voice thick with emotion.

"No," she answered, sure he had deliberately avoided any mention of his brother.

"When I found out where he was based we kept in touch. We managed a couple of days together in London. He'd been flying a lot of missions. I could tell he was tired, needed a rest."

Bonnie knew from his voice the telling was hard. She wanted to climb under the covers and close her ears.

"Do you think you could get a leave and we could go somewhere for a week?" I asked him.

"I hadn't noticed that the war was over," he shot back sarcastically.

"I knew from his tone, so unlike him, how weary he was and how he wished the war was really over."

"London wasn't much more than a pile of rubble and still the bombs kept falling. We were in a pub, working at enjoying the warm, English beer. Linus put down his glass and suggested we find a place where there was some excitement, and maybe some real booze."

"But we didn't go looking for excitement or booze. Instead, we ended up sitting on a pile of rubble, talking about home, about some of the things we did as kids and about the red car. For a moment there was a trace of debonair, happy-go-lucky Linus we all knew, as he wondered about some of the girls he used to date, especially Carrie who wrote to him regularly. He talked about Dad, smiling, shaking his head, saying how different he was from other fathers."

Alex's sentences were choppy, with long pauses.

"Whoever gets home first can take the car out, wake the town up" Linus joked and wondered if the horn would still work.

"Remember how mom hated that horn," he said with a grin that was more sad than happy. "He was doing his best to be lighthearted, but I couldn't help but feel the that the red car was no longer important to him."

Alex stopped talking, got dressed, put on his coat and went out. He was gone all day.

It was late when he returned and he was cold. Bonnie rubbed his hands, then pressed her warm ones against his cold cheeks. His beard was scratchy and there was a weariness about him that made Bonnie wonder if he had been walking all day. "Can I fix you something, Alex?" she offered.

"I've had dinner," he told her.

Bonnie stood waiting for him to say more, but he took off his coat, hung it in the closet and told her, "We'll talk tomorrow, Bonnie, I'm pretty tired."

He bent and kissed her. "We'll talk tomorrow, he repeated, then added, "I love you, Bonnie."

Alex was undressed, in bed and asleep while Bonnie was left to wonder what tomorrow would bring.

Bonnie was in the kitchen when Alex came to join her the next morning. "Hungry?" she asked.

"For now, I'll settle for coffee," he told her, tussling her hair on the way to the table. Bonnie filled two mugs and sat across from him. "You look rested," she said. The weariness was gone but the seriousness of yesterday was still there.

"I haven't slept like that since I was a kid," he told her. "And now, I have something very important to discuss with you. I want us to get married, Bonnie, soon."

Bonnie couldn't help but smile at the sudden urgency.

"Did someone accuse you of living in sin?" she asked.

"No, nothing like that," he said, not even smiling at her remark. "But I wondered what we were waiting for, Bonnie. We've always known we would marry when I came home and now I'm home, I want you to be my wife."

Bonnie reached for his hand. "Alex, I think it's a wonderful idea. What do you mean by soon?" she asked.

"Today, Tomorrow. How long does it take?"

"A week, probably."

"Can we get started today?" he asked. And still amused at the urgency in his voice, Bonnie told him, "We can talk to your father about blood tests. I think that's where we start."

"Mom and dad will be delighted that we're getting married," Alex told Bonnie. "They're probably a little upset with me taking off the way I did."

"Perhaps, perhaps not," Bonnie said thoughtfully, then suggested to Alex, "Don't you think we should spend the next few days with them while we plan our wedding?"

Alex groaned, then agreed.

"Home can be a strange place when you've been away for a while," Alex said, "especially away doing something as unnatural as fighting a war. You expect your family to see a change in you, at least notice how you've matured. But they treat you as though nothing has changed."

"And mom and dad, you wonder how much they'll have changed, but they seem the same as always."

"Are you sure, Alex?" Bonnie asked. "I don't think so. Not them or anyone else. The war has taken its toll on everyone. The pain of losing Linus, the day to day worry about you, your father alone to care for the sick of the entire county. No, Alex, they aren't the same, any more than you're the same."

"I guess we soldiers think the war was fought on one side of the world only. I have to say I'm ashamed," Alex admitted.

"The pain of losing Linus must be terrible for them, especially for dad," he said, and ashamed of the shallowness of his words, the relationship between Linus and his dad was suddenly very real to him.

"Linus was fun-loving, happy-go-lucky. He seemed always to

live for today. And Dad, so different, so serious. Living in the present, but always seeming to reach into the past. And yet, different as they were, Linus and dad, there was something special between them."

"Once, way back when we were kids," Alex continued, "we were wondering what to get dad for Father's Day… I suggested saving our allowance and paying someone to build a new bench."

"Linus was shocked. He made it plain that Dad's bench wasn't something you replaced, ever."

"When we were kids, we'd sit on the bench with Dad and he'd tell us stories. They were always about his grandfather, an immigrant who came from far, far away, to a country so big only the sea was bigger, to own a piece of land all his own. There were dozens of stories, all different and Dad would make them exciting, but more important, they were all stories told to Dad as he and his Grandpa sat together on the same bench. When his grandfather died, Dad took the bench home and it has been with him ever since, and here I was suggesting we get rid of it."

"Linus understood about dad and the bench. I didn't. To me, it was just an old wooden bench."

Alex sat, thoughtful again, and his words, when he spoke, were barely audible.

"Linus had been popping up in my mind more than usual," he said, his voice getting thick again, "and I had dreams, some of them terrible. It was Linus and me in London. Linus and me sitting on a pile of rubble. Linus talking about home, and the red car. Linus not coming home." Bonnie saw tears in his eyes as he continued.

"It was a terrible night. Not even the terrors of the battlefield gave me such nightmares."

"I know," Bonnie told him. "You were all over the bed, calling Linus's name, sometimes other names I didn't recognize. I was afraid to wake you up so I went and sat in the living room until you stopped dreaming."

"I'm sorry," he apologized, "leaving like I did yesterday, Bonnie. But I needed to be alone. There's an emptiness at home without Linus. Mom and Dad don't mention him. But I knew I had to deal with… let myself remember him, not as he was in London, weary, mentally and physically exhausted, but the Linus I grew up with."

"I walked and walked and when I found a grassy spot by the river, I sat on the bank of the river and let the memories come. I laughed, out loud sometimes, and I cried a little, and after a while, I just sat, watching the water as it rushed past me. Undeterred by the rocks in its path, it kept right on moving forward, and watching it I knew it was time for me to move on with my life, yours and mine, to accept what I couldn't change."

Reaching for Bonnie's hand, Alex continued, "I started thinking about us, how I wanted to marry, soon, and I wanted to tell you about the plans I had for our life together."

"I didn't expect you to have plans so soon," Bonnie told him, surprised.

Suddenly, Alex was telling her about London, describing the devastation, telling her about the buildings, old as antiquity, being held together with a few bricks, ready to collapse in a windstorm.

Listening to him, Bonnie hoped he wasn't planning on going to London to haul away bricks and piles of rubble and look for ways to shore up old buildings. "And what did all this have to do with his plans for them?" she wondered.

As Alex continued with his description of destruction, Bonnie began to suspect that somewhere in this detailed account of war-torn London lay his plans.

"I know Dad hoped that after the war he'd be able to talk me into being a doctor, but being a doctor never appealed to me. I didn't know what I wanted to do with my life. Now I do. I've known since that night with Linus."

Bonnie sat holding her breath.

"I've decided to be an architect," he said.

"An architect, Alex?" Bonnie said. She couldn't help it if she reacted as though he was speaking a strange language.

Alex's only acknowledgement that he heard her was to squeeze her hand and smile as he began to explain his plans.

"There's going to be a demand for architects as the rebuilding work begins, and there'll be opportunities for young architects with nothing more than a college degree to work with the best architects in the world. Imagine being a part of such a mammoth undertaking, Bonnie," Alex concluded excitedly.

"What mammoth undertaking?" Bonnie asked. "You spent four years fighting to bring peace to the world. Isn't that enough? Let them rebuild." There was an edge to her voice as she reminded him, "You just got home, Alex."

"Bonnie, I'm talking about after college, not now," and then he was pleading. "If you could see it, cities in ruins, people without homes, the tragedies and sadness of war all around them. They're going to need help. They can't do it alone."

Bonnie sat staring. "I need time to think about this," she told him. "Being an architect sounds great, if that's what you want, but rebuilding the world? Right now, it seems a little extreme to me."

"It' not the world, Bonnie. It's just a few cities… I guess I sound a little foolish."

Bonnie reached across the table for his hand and pressing it against her cheek, assured him. "Not foolish, Alex, but you've only been home such a short time and we have so much catching up to do. Suddenly I'm bombarded by an idea that's strange, different. You have a few years of school ahead of you, plenty of time to work this out."

"I'm looking ahead too fast, too far," Alex said, hoping to reassure her. "Let's go tell your family and mine about our plans to get married."

"How about breakfast first?" Bonnie suggested.

As she went about preparing it, she asked Alex about his sisters.

"You've hardly mentioned them. What did you think about them after not seeing them for such a long time?"

"They were so happy to have me home. Now maybe life will begin around here," Lucy told me.

"But they've changed, Bonnie. I expected a big change in Lucy, but Emma surprised me. She's lost the gypsy look. The Vokil look has been softened by the Hersey genes and Grandma Dole's too. She's much more attractive than she realizes. But right now, she's so uptight that if the doorbell doesn't ring soon with Paul on the other side, she's going to crack. By the way, do you know this guy Emma's stuck on?" Alex asked.

"Sure, I know him, and so do you," Bonnie said. "He was only a year behind us, but had different interests... mostly girls. He's a real Don Juan, good looking, drove an expensive car... He dated Emma a few times and the next thing I heard he was off to war."

"With her brother leaving and all their friends stopping to say goodbye, I think Emma got caught up in the war mania, someone to say goodbye to, someone to promise to love forever. I have to admit I was surprised at Emma, but as I said, he was a Don Juan and Emma was only sixteen."

"Really impressed with him, aren't you," Alex remarked.

Bonnie shrugged. "He'll be home soon. We'll see how grown up he is. About your other sister. A big change there, you said."

"Probably the biggest shock since I got home." Admitted. "When I left, she was a cute, giggly fourteen-year-old. Now, she's eighteen and beautiful. She can't wait for the ships and the planes to bring the boys home. She wants to date them all. Actually, Lucy's a lot of fun. She reminds me of Linus. We talked about Linus. She told me she moved into his bedroom, slept in his bed and cried every night for a long time."

"I miss him," she told me sadly.

"Lucy was the only one who could talk about how she felt.

Mom and Emma will, eventually, but not Dad. I doubt if he ever will."

They sat eating breakfast, the earlier strain on their relationship gone for now, following the conversation wherever it took them. There was so much to catch up on.

36

Back home later that day, Karl was delighted to see his son. Annie greeted his return with a smile and a hug and invited them for dinner. "A nice fat, stuffed chicken, a gift from one of your father's patients," she told them.

"Sorry I took off like that," Alex told his parents, "but I was edgy and restless…"

"And needed to be with Bonnie," his father interjected.

Alex was pleased with his father's easy acceptance of his absence and followed him willingly when he suggested they go outside. "We can visit a little while the women prepare dinner," he said as he led Alex out to the bench.

Settled on the bench, Karl smiled broadly at his son and said, "And now?"

Alex wasn't sure how to answer his father's "and now" and told him, "It's strange being home, Dad. One day you're on the battlefield, worried whether you'll be alive by nightfall and the next thing you know you're thrust into a completely different situation where you're not only alive, but your whole life is on front of you, just waiting for you to decide what you want to do with it."

"Life is like that, Alex," his father said quietly. "Sometimes it changes in your favor, sometimes not."

"This time in my favor, wouldn't you say," Alex asked.

"Yes, in your favor, son," he agreed, his hand on his son's knee, patting it affectionately. Then he asked the question that was uppermost in his mind. "Now tell me, Alex, have you made any decisions about your future or is it too soon to settle such important issues?"

Alex was uncomfortable, wishing he didn't have to disappoint his father. "For the time being, it'll be back to school," he said in a deliberate offhand manner.

His father wasn't fooled. "I can tell it's not good news by the way you're being evasive," he told him.

"How do you know its not good news?" Alex asked, irritated. "The only news you want to hear is that I'm going to be a doctor. Anything else is bad news."

Immediately sorry for the harshness of his words, Alex apologized. "It's just that being a doctor has never appealed to me, Dad."

"Tell me about your plans, Alex. I promise never to mention doctor to you again." Karl hadn't tried to hide disappointment but it was a touch of sarcasm that angered Alex.

"I've been thinking I'd like to be an architect." He told his father, making no attempt to soften the blow.

Karl gave his son a blank look. "I don't think I've said the word architect more than once in my life. It's almost not in my vocabulary. What do you want to design, houses?" he asked, not even pretending interest.

"No, not houses," Alex said gruffly, then hoping to make his father understand, Alex tried to explain the ruins, the devastation in London and Europe.

"But that's what happens in war. They will rebuild, not us. We defeated that monster Hitler and helped bring peace to the world, isn't that enough?" Karl said, echoing Bonnie's words.

"Well, I have a few years of schooling ahead of me, Dad," Alex reminded his father, anxious to get off the subject of his future.

Karl sat gazing off at the wind-swept yard, his lips clamped hard together. When he spoke again, Alex knew his father was trying to hold back his anger.

"Your horizons are wider than mine, son," he told him. "Those of us who stayed home relied on newsreels to keep us informed. That's a lot different from being there, being part of it. I knew the bombs were being dropped, killing, destroying. We could see it all at the movie theater. I went only once. The sounds of war are terrible and I had to leave. The mind is not conditioned to such horrors, so much hatred. And always, there was the knowledge that my sons were there, and my fear for them."

Karl was suddenly quiet and Alex knew his father was thinking of Linus. When he spoke, the anger was muted though still there.

"The need to rebuild... that's a new thought you've introduced me to. I need to think about it, Alex. But, in the meantime, I'll practice saying architect until it rolls easy off the tongue."

Alex was stunned by his father's sarcasm, and not sure how to move the conversation away from his plans, he simply told him, "I'm sorry you don't approve, Dad."

"It isn't as easy for me to forgive as it seems to be for you," Karl told Alex, and getting up off the bench, he turned his face to his son, and his black eyes fierce with bitterness, his voice sharp as a rapier, he told him, "I have no pity for those responsible for your brother's death. That much will never change," and turned and walked away from him toward the house. When he reached the door, he turned and told Alex, "Come, we'll see if dinner's ready." Relieved at this small peace offering, Alex followed his father in the house.

There was a festive air at diner once Bonnie and Alex announced their plans to marry.

"Just family," Bonnie told them. "Yours and mine."

Annie saw the hard look of anger in her husband's eyes and realized he was struggling to regain his composure. She looked over at Alex. He avoided her eyes. Later, when Karl told his wife of their son's plans, she too was appalled.

37

Ten days later, Bonnie and Alex were married, not by the Justice of the Peace as Alex would have liked it, but in the church Bonnie had attended with her parents while growing up.

A week later, Paul came home.

Emma, preparing to leave for her father's office, stood staring at the man striding up the path to her front door.

"Paul?" she questioned, half aloud, hardly believing her eyes, then ran to open the door.

"Emma," he hollered ecstatically, and before she knew what was happening, she was in his arms. "Emma, Emma," he repeated as he showered her with kisses.

"Oh Paul, I can't believe it's you. I can't believe you're home," Emma said, finding it hard to believe he was really there, that it was his arms around her.

It was a wild few minutes. They laughed and kissed and hugged until Emma pushed him away. "Let me look at you, Paul," she said as she examined him from head to toe.

"You look wonderful. You're taller, a lot taller," she told him as she stood admiring him.

"That's the first thing my mother said," he told her.

"You're older looking too and quite handsome," Emma said as she continued her examination of him.

Paul laughed and twirled her around. "You look just like I knew you would, only more so," he told her.

"What's more so?" Emma asked, feeling as giddy as a teenage on her first date.

"More everything… more beautiful, more beautiful and more beautiful," Paul told her.

Emma basked in it all, every word.

Paul looked around the room, peered into the dining room and finally asked, "Where is everybody?"

"Mom and Lucy will be here shortly. Dad's at the office which is where I belong. But not today. Oh, Paul, I can't believe you're home," she said as they stood smiling at each other.

They heard a car door slam and Paul watched out the window as Emma's mother walked toward the house.

"I'm sorry about Linus," Paul told Emma.

"My parents are still trying to accept it," she told him, "and now with the boys coming home, it's very hard for them."

The door opened and Lucy came bounding in.

"Whose beautiful car is that parked in front of our house?" she asked, her eyes going from Emma and resting on Paul.

"You remember my sister, Lucy, don't you Paul," Emma said.

For a few seconds he stared, glancing at one to the other, then shook his head in wonder. "Look who's all grown up," he said.

"Well, almost, but not quite," Annie said as she gave Paul a warm greeting. "We're so happy to see you, Paul. It's been a long war."

"Emma wrote about Linus. I'm so sorry, Mrs. Vokil," Paul told her.

"Thank you," she said quietly and suggested they have something to drink, "ice tea or soda," she offered.

"I was thinking of asking Emma to take me to see all the old hangouts, our favorite spots," Paul said.

"It'll be interesting to get acquainted with the town again."

"Not much has changed," Annie told him. "But you'll enjoy finding that out for yourself."

Lucy watched them walk hand in hand, down the path to the car. "I don't remember him being that good looking," Lucy told her mother.

"I doubt if you even noticed him back then, Lucy. You were too busy with friends your own age," her mother reminded as she headed for the kitchen. "I'm going to make a pot of tea. Would you like a cup?" she asked and was surprised when her daughter came to join her.

"None of the guys I went to school with are home yet. Either that or I don't recognize the way I didn't recognize Paul," Lucy told her mother. "I feel so out of place, Mom. A part of my life got wiped away. Where do I fit in?" she asked in a forlorn tone, so unlike her.

"A part of your life didn't get wiped away, Lucy," her mother assured her. "In a way it was just put on hold, the same as everyone else's. Things will fall onto place, but it will take time."

Abruptly, Lucy changed the subject. "He really is handsome, isn't he?" she said, and what Annie heard was no casual observation.

Annie turned to look at her daughter, young, beautiful, and so eager to get her life moving.

"Please didn't spoil it for Emma by flirting with Paul," she cautioned her. Her mother's words went unheeded. Lucy couldn't keep her eyes of Paul. She couldn't convince herself that Paul belonged to Emma, especially when his eyes seemed always to be searching for hers.

As the days passed, they forgot about Emma as Lucy flirted unmercifully. Paul fell under her spell, and captivated by her beauty, thrilled by her undisguised pleasure in him, his eyes followed her every move as Lucy, recklessly and deliberately, helped Emma fade from his memory. Every part of her responded to his touch and when, at last Paul kissed her, Emma's fate was irrevocably sealed.

For Emma, it was no contest. Before she was aware that her sister had her sights on Paul, he was under her spell.

Will Thornton, visiting the Vokils, anxious to welcome Paul home, watched incredulously as Lucy deliberately stole her sister's beau. Not hiding his disapproval, Will told Lucy, "Aren't you over-doing the welcome?"

"Am I?' she asked innocently, giving Will one of her sweetest smiles.

Will talked to Paul. It was too late.

"Don't think I don't know I'm a cad," he admitted without the least bit of remorse. "For Lucy I'd go back and fight another war."

"He sounds like a lovesick teenager, not someone home from a war," Will told himself.

"Perhaps that's the problem, his and Lucy's. They haven't had a chance to experience those lovesick, teenage years, and finding themselves attracted to each other, they're sure it's love."

Will worried about Emma.

The thrill of Paul being home eclipsed everything going on around Emma, so that when he broke the news to her, she simply started, then asked, "What did you say, Paul?"

Paul had prepared his little speech and delivered it, not pre-pared for Emma's stunned reaction. When he had to repeat it, he found himself stammering, "I hope you'll forgive me Emma. I have something to tell you... Lucy and I are going to be married."

"Your marrying my sister?" Emma asked in disbelief.

When his answer was a nod, Emma turned and ran up the stairs.

The effects of Lucy's betrayal cast a spell over the Vokil house-hold. Emma accused her parents, especially her mother of turning a blind eye to Lucy's deceptiveness.

"You were here when I was at work," she accused her mother. She's your daughter. You've never been able to see past her looks. You've seen how she acts when there's a guy around... flirting, teasing, rolling those big, blue eyes of hers, and you thought it was cute, didn't you? Why didn't you do something when you saw her playing it up to Paul?"

Annie had never heard Emma lash out at anyone the away she was going after her, and heartsick as she was, she had no words to soften her daughter's anger.

"I'm sorry, Emma, but what makes you so sure I could have changed anything?" she asked. "Remember, you were very young when Paul went away. People change." Annie knew any attempt to reconcile Emma to the sad outcome, would, in Emma's mind, be a way of defending not only Lucy but herself as well.

Until the day Lucy and Paul were married, Emma was not a part of the Vokil household. She kept to her room when she was not at work. For weeks she tortured herself, reading and rereading Paul's letters, remembering his last days at home.

How many times did she hear his last words to her, "write me, Emma. Wait for me." The words rang in her ears and haunted her, until gaunt and haggard, her father took a firm stand with her.

He handed her a bottle of pills and told her, "Take these, Emma, before you collapse. Dying isn't going to change anything."

When he kept her, making sure she was taking the pills and eating properly, he told her, "You've done enough weeping and hating, Emma. There's other fish out there. Go after one."

At times her father drove her crazy with his solicitude and worn out platitudes, but Emma knew that without his caring, her recovery might never have been complete.

38

Will Thornton, struggling to establish an accounting business in Lockview, made it a habit to stop at Vokils to check on Emma. She appreciated his concern, but it was close to a year before she agreed to go to the movies with him and she was surprised at how much she enjoyed the evening.

Having spent the war years in college where the war was not always the topic of conversation, but rather the world after the war, Will was excited about the possibilities for the future.

"The world as we've always known it is changing," he told Emma. "The coming years will see advancements none of us dreamed possible. For now, just getting the country back on a peace time economy means there will be opportunities for millions."

Will's enthusiasm was contagious and Emma found herself listening intently, enjoying and gradually taking part, not only in the conversations but in the world around her.

"He's like a breath of fresh air," Emma told herself. "He's helped brush away the cobb webs I let gather while I mooned over my loss."

"When he talks about tomorrow, I know he hopes to include me, but it's still too soon to think about trusting myself to anyone."

Dr. Vokil did not share in the opportunities that Will Thornton as so enthusiastic about. Struggling to care for an ever-expanding population, he told his wife one day, "The only difference between my early years in practice is that now when I make house calls, instead of a horse and buggy, I have a car."

Karl expected Roger Carstairs to walk in any day and pick up his practice where he left off three years ago, but when he did come, it was only to collect a few personal belongings and to let Karl know he planned on going back to Med School to become a surgeon.

"The war really broadened my concept of medicine," he told Karl. "I was in a makeshift hospital where there never seemed to be a lull in the fighting, and the casualties were being brought in faster than we could take care of them. I was doing things I hadn't learned in Med School or Farmington. Our only concern was to save lives, working without the needed experience, medicine or equipment, reaching into our memory for something we'd read or heard discussed at the hospital, anything to keep the wounded alive until they could be taken to a regular hospital."

"To come back to the mundane problems of a small town," Roger continued, "to winter sniffles, colicky babies, over protective mothers." He shook his head. "It would be anticlimactic, drive me crazy," he concluded, not even noticing Annie glaring at him.

Karl knew Roger wasn't trying to belittle his practice, making the problems of Farmington seem inconsequential. He understood the contrast, the after you've seen Paree syndrome, but even as he congratulated him, wishing him well, Roger's decision was especially disappointing.

"Everybody's talking about changes," Karl told Annie after Roger had left. "I'm happy for everything that's being done to help the boys coming home, the opportunity for Roger to become a surgeon, but what about those of us who have struggled through the hardships here at home, and are still struggling."

"Suppose I write a letter to the government to remind them that I've had to make do for years, and that I'm not on anyone's priority list for replacements. If I told them that my stethoscope is being held together with electrical tape, that the sterilizer in my office is a pan of boiling water with antiseptic added, and that my supply of medicine isn't much more than aspirin and that the typewriter in my office sounds like a runaway truck. Would they send out a representative to take my order for the latest equipment?"

When Karl complained, Annie knew how tired he was, and not just desperate for new equipment but for a doctor to share the load, but she had little comfort to offer. Their lives had settled into a pattern of acceptance. Karl accepted that he had to plug along until he was fortunate enough to find an assistant and he knew no amount of griping would replace his worn-out equipment. Roger had promised to keep an eye out for a doctor interested in a rural practice, but Karl knew that even with the men and women in Med School under the G.I. Bill there would be opportunities offered to them in cities throughout the country and the rural territories would be sadly overlooked.

"Well Annie, there's hope for us yet," Karl told his wife when he came home for dinner. "A catalogue came in the mail today with page after page of shiny equipment. I gave it to Emma and told her to order the things we use every day by the dozen and two of everything else."

Annie hadn't heard so much pleasure in her husband's voice in a long time. Later, when she went to join him on the bench, he handed her the newspaper.

"Look at all the ads for things that didn't even exist last year," he said.

Amused at how little attention her husband seemed to pay to progress, Annie told him, "A little longer than last year, Karl. The war's been over for four years."

"How quickly time passes," Karl said, folding the paper and putting it on his lap, he asked his wife, "Do you remember the day we went shopping for our first car, Annie?"

"I'll always remember that day," Annie said, grinning. "You kissed me in front of the salesman who sold us the car."

Karl chuckled at the memory. "What say we go shopping for a

new car on Saturday?" he suggested. "I'll tell Emma not to make any appointments."

Thrilled, Emma told him, "Let's not get a dark color this time."

"We'll get any color you want as long as you let me kiss you in front of the salesman," Karl promised.

"Let's go to Buffalo,' Annie suggested. "They'll have more to choose from."

"And go out to dinner," Karl said, grinning at Annie's cry for pleasure.

Karl, out shopping for a new car, became aware for the first time of the changes not only in the automobile showrooms filled with cars, but in the shops and stores where there seemed to be an endless supply of everything the heart desired.

"Where have I been while all this was going on?" he asked his wife as she led him through one of the new department stores.

"Tucked away in Farmington, taking care of the sick," she told him. "Besides, you were never one to shop," she reminded him.

If Karl had been slow to recognize the tempo of progress in the post war world, Will Thornton was not.

"No country that can furnish the world with the armaments of war in such quantity and so quickly is going to let its factories sit idle," Will had told Emma one evening as they sat over a snack after a movie.

He had been right, of course.

While education took a prominent place in the post-war years, with President Truman's G.I. Bill sending thousands of young men, home from the battlefield to college, progress in other areas was literally leaping ahead, changing the way people lived their lives with an array of goods that dazzled the eyes. As cars began to fill the showrooms with a choice of colors and models, for women it was a shopper's paradise as racks of new fabrics were introduced. Orlon and nylon replaced cotton and wool, and when polyester was introduced, the pronunciation had to be learned as well as its meaning.

The old wringer washing machine took its place in the relic heap as automatic washers took their place in the average house-hold, and not long after, clothes flapping in the wind gradually disappeared as the automatic dryer took its place alongside the automatic washer. Every year something new was introduced as progress moved relentlessly along.

Will Thornton, with his college degree and his CPA license, had eagerly anticipated the quick changes in the business world.

"For every business making a dollar, Uncle Sam will be waiting for his share. My job will be to help him get it," he had told Emma. She had laughed at his seriousness, while at the same time admiring his foresight and eagerness, not doubting for a minute his ability to do just that.

Now, together again one evening, at the same restaurant, hav-ing a snack after a movie, Will was telling Emma about the prog-ress he was making.

"This is just what you planned a long time ago, isn't it?" she asked him.

"I suppose in a way it is," Will admitted. "But for a while I just knew what I wasn't going to do when the army tuned me down."

"And that was?" Emma asked.

"That I wasn't going to work in a factory," Will admitted a bit sheepishly. Chalk it up to immaturity, but it was my way of getting revenge."

Emma sat looking at him, not saying anything.

Will felt the need to explain.

"You have no idea how humiliating it was to stand stark naked in front of a hundred guys, be told you're a reject and have a gruff voice tell you, move along, keep moving. If you can't pass the phys-ical, you're not treated like a human being."

Emma tried to be sympathetic and tried not to laugh, but the picture was too graphic. She couldn't help herself.

Suddenly the humor of it struck Will and he began to laugh. "It's the first time I ever saw the humor in it," he told Emma. It was times like this, laughing together at the past, talking about the future, that made them aware of the closeness of their relationship.

Will sat looking at Emma. "She seems so lighthearted when we're together. Have the wounds healed? Would she marry me if I asked her?"

These were questions on his mind whenever he was with her, he realized.

And Emma, still smiling, was thinking how empty her life would be without Will. "But is it love or is it dependency? He's always been there to help me through the rough times."

Driving home, they passed a subdivision of new houses half built.

"I can't believe how fast whole areas are expanding, Emma told Will. "Who's going to live in all those houses?"

"They're probably already sold," he told her.

"I wouldn't want to live on a street where the houses are all the same," she said. "And look how bare the landscape is. They've cut down all the trees."

"It's sad isn't it," Will agreed. "It's called progress," he added with a touch of cynicism. But where would you want to live?" he asked.

"In a house where the trees haven't all been chopped down and where there are no fences to make strangers of people and where there's a big yard for children to play."

"Well Emma, if you'd consent to marry me, I'd search the countryside for just the right house," Will told her.

"I wondered if I'd ever trust my life to anyone," Emma said, "but tonight I was thinking how empty my life would be without you, Will."

"Can I take that to be a yes answer?" Will asked.

When Emma told him yes, Will was momentarily speechless. "I feel as if there should be something more momentous about our decision, maybe a speech telling you how much I love you."

"Or maybe a proposal on bended knee," Emma suggested, laughing. But their kiss was momentous enough to make up for the lack of declarations.

Emma's mother was beside herself with happiness and plans. Her father said, "It's about time."

When Emma said, "a small wedding, Mom," her mother groaned in disappointment, and her father nodded approval.

Later, when they were alone, Annie asked her daughter, "Does your wanting a small wedding have anything to do with Lucy?"

Angered by her mother's question, in a tone that startled her, "Absolutely not!" and turned to go upstairs.

Shaken by Emma's abruptness at the mention of Lucy, Annie was determined not to let the past interfere with Emma's happiness and her wedding plans.

Emma was half way up the stairs when Annie called to her, "Could we have a cup of tea together and talk about this?" she asked, near tears.

Emma stopped. She stood rubbing a finger along the bannister, back and forth across the dark wood, then turned and slowly came back down to join her mother.

"I'm sorry, Emma," Annie apologized. "I shouldn't have mentioned Lucy."

In a quiet but firm voice, Emma told her mother, "Mentioning Lucy doesn't bother me, Mom, but it made me angry that you think Lucy could influence the plans for my wedding."

Annie apologized again as she prepared the tea.

"It's okay, Mom," Emma said calmly. "I know that Lucy's left Paul and is going to divorce him, that she left for Reno two days ago and won't be here for the wedding. I'm sorry the marriage didn't work out, but my life is not affected by it. Perhaps after Lucy has her divorce and Paul is no longer a part of her life, we can be friends again."

Annie wiped a tear from her cheek, and Emma, wondering how many tears her mother had shed over Lucy and her unhappy marriage, reached over and put her arm around her mother's shoulder.

"We'll work it out, Mom," Emma told her. "For now, let's worry about making an invitation list for my wedding."

Will and Emma chose New York City for their honeymoon.

"I don't really want to stand holding hands and watch water tumbling over the falls.," Emma told Will when he asked where she'd like to go. "I've already seen that, I'd like to go somewhere where we see things and do things, we might never have a chance to do for years and years."

"How about New York City?" he asked her.

"I'd love it," Emma said.

"I've already made reservations," Will told her, amused and delighted with the surprise on her face.

"Oh, Will," she said, smiling happily, "we're going to have a wonderful life together."

39

The small clapboard church was filling up quickly, heightened by an air of expectancy as the ushers escorted family members to their seats and the ringing of the church bell announced the arrival of the bride.

With the strains of the wedding march filling the church, Emma, holding lightly to her father's arm, started up the aisle, her dark eyes fixed on Will, a smile on her lips as she advanced toward him.

As Karl escorted his daughter down the aisle, memories of the other times he'd walked down this aisle flashed through his mind.

He'd walked his mother down this aisle a long time ago. She'd worn a blue gown that matched her eyes and he'd worn his first suit that wasn't out of the catalogue. He'd been proud and happy to be giving his mother to a man he knew would make her happy.

A few years later, he stood spellbound as his beautiful bride walked toward him. It was the most important day of his life. Annie, how he loved her. And now Emma.

"We've shared sadness and tragedies these past years," he thought, but as he walked down the aisle with her, sharing in her happiness, he was reminded of Mitch and his assurance that there was magic in life.

In New York City, Emma and Will were typical tourists. They climbed the steps to the top of the Empire State Building and gazed in awe at the city, then came back at night when the city was all lit up.

Emma begged Will to take her to Radio City Music Hall to see the Rockettes a second time. "They're absolutely fabulous. Not a single one out of step," she told him at least half a dozen times.

When they boarded the ferry for a trip to the Statue of Liberty, Will told her, "This is a one-time trip."

Laughing, Emma hugged his arm. "Once will do it," she promised, "but we do have to see it. Do you know that statue wasn't here when my great grandfather came to America?"

"Mine either," Will said. "They came over on the Mayflower."

"Really." Emma was impressed.

"Just kidding, Emma. You've heard their accents. They came from Scotland just before my brother Ed was born." Will leaned over and kissed her, "I love you Emma," He told her "and I love the way you believe everything I tell you." He grinned when she walked away from him, pretending to be offended.

Emma stood at the rail of the ferry, gazing up at the statue. "It's so majestic, so impressive, so welcoming. I'm going to ask your parents how they felt when they first spied it," she told Will.

Later in the day, she reminded Will that they hadn't been to Rockefeller Center. "We should go and skate around the rink at least once," she insisted.

Will groaned when he realized Emma was serious about skating but her enthusiasm was contagious and he found he was enjoying himself as hand in hand, they glided across the ice until the music stopped and out of breath, they found a bench and sat to watch the other skaters flying past them.

It was a quiet moment, the music began again, a waltz. Emma hummed along with the music. Will moved closer and put his arm around her. Emma turned and smiled at him. "I never thought life would ever be like this, Will," she told him, then asked him, "Do you remember how you used to come to cheer me up? Dad always said I was fine to live with, a least for a while, after you'd been there."

"Emma, I didn't just come to cheer you up," Will told her. "I was in love with you." He reached for her hand and pulled her up off the bench. "Let's skate a couple more times around and chase away the shadows, then go find a place where we can get a hot chocolate."

The shadows were quickly chased away and the past forgotten as Will and Emma joined the skaters. A gentle breeze that ruffled their hair had taken the past and carried it away.

40

For Dr. Karl Vokil there was no gentle breeze or soft music to help chase away the problems of caring for the sick of Farmington and the county. And the rift between him and Alex, though not quite the open wound it had been, had not entirely healed. Not the Marshall Plan or the opportunity for Alex to work with a group of prestigious architects had convinced Karl that it was America's responsibility to rebuild the war-torn cities. Alex's talk of humanitarianism and reconciliation fell on deaf ears and their goodbyes held more than a touch of resentment.

Bonnie's early misgivings about rebuilding war torn cities were quickly forgotten when Alex received the invitation to join a group of architects leaving for London just a week after his graduation. The Marshall Plan had convinced her that her husband was, in her words, "a visionary," and she couldn't pack their bags fast enough.

"I'll only be a beginner, Bonnie," Alex had reminded his wife, "following orders, assigned to the simplest tasks, but it's the opportunity of a lifetime."

Alex tried to prepare Bonnie for the shocks ahead, but he made no excuses for the apartment assigned to them. "It's not the cozy, little apartment we're used to, but it's in surprisingly good condition" and he was proud of her when, after she examined it, she told him, "I think we'll be quite comfortable here."

Annie sat reading Bonnie's latest letter. From the beginning of their sojourn, she had written regularly, aware, but ignoring the rift between Alex and his father. They had parted with Alex pretending to understand his father's stubborn attitude more than he did.

"London is a long way from here," he told his mother. "Fences aren't easily mended by mail."

"It's not just stubbornness, Alex," she told him. "And it's not entirely about Linus, either. I don't think you realize how hard it will be for your father, for both of us, having a son so far away, never seeing you and Bonnie."

"Life has been rather hard on your Dad these last few years, carrying the load alone since all those doctors went off to war and none of them interested in coming to practice in a rural community," Annie reminded her son.

But Bonnie's letters were so full of the many facets of their life, Annie felt closer to them now the she had been during the year Alex had been in college.

"We have a small apartment that back home might have be considered a tenement," Bonnie had written in her first letter. There are no gaping holes but it has been damaged, not by a direct hit but the shaking it took from bombs falling around it. But it's comfortable and there's another American family doing the same work as Alex, so we aren't entirely among strangers."

Bonnie wrote about her visits to the age old buildings still standing, with just a few gaping holes, and the thrill of watching the progress as the buildings were being put back together.

Another time she wrote of their stunned surprise when the Russians sealed off Berlin. We are still in awe as the Berlin Airlift continues to show America's determination to resist the communist threat.

Later she wrote she was going to have a child, and Karl suffered through her pregnancy. "She should have the baby at home," he insisted.

They called their son Joey, sent pictures and kept them up to date on his progress.

"We keep waiting to hear that a new doctor has arrived so you and dad can take a vacation and come to visit us. You'd love London," Bonnie wrote invitingly.

"One of these days," Annie told her, as she folded the letter and put it on the buffet where Karl would find it.

Karl came home, tired as usual, saw the letter from Bonnie, and took it outside to read while there was still a bit of daylight.

Bonnie's letter took the edge off the resentment Karl felt toward his son. "If she keeps writing, she'll have me convinced Annie and I should start packing our bags," he told himself as he took the letter out of the envelope.

"We both need a change," Karl told himself after reading Bonnie's latest invitation. "Annie's prowling around this big house as lonely as I am. We have a grandson we've never seen. Joey, Karl said with a longing. Did they name him for my Grandpa? I bet they did." Karl felt the warmth of their love for him as each letter brought him closer to regretting his unwillingness to share instead of condemning his son's choice of a career.

"Who's ever thought that after raising four children we'd find ourselves so alone?" Karl sighed as he folded the letter and put it back in the envelope. "Emma comes often, but two young sons keep her busy. And Lucy..." Karl could feel his anger rising at the very thought of Lucy's marriage ruined by a gigolo who couldn't stick to the girl he couldn't wait to get into bed with. "That's all he wanted, didn't know the first thing about love. But then, neither did Lucy," Karl was forced to admit.

"Why didn't we lock her up until she came to her senses?" Karl asked himself for the hundredth time, and the answer was always the same. "She'd have climbed out the window."

Annie called him to dinner and Lucy still on his mind, he asked Annie, "Have you talked to Lucy lately?"

"She called last night after you went to bed," Annie told him. "Other than talking about how well her business is doing, how much she enjoys living where the weather is always warm and how much she likes Las Vegas, she didn't say much else."

"And nothing about a visit home?" Karl asked.

"No, not a word," Annie said.

"I get the strangest feeling there's something going on in her life that makes her want to stay there," Karl said. "Do you think there's a man in her life?"

"All I can say is that she's different from the girl who went to Reno for a divorce. She sounds happy. There's no anger or bitterness or tears like there used to be that first year. But she doesn't tell us much about her private life so there's not much to speculate about," Annie concluded.

Karl was sorry he'd mentioned Lucy. Her marriage, her divorce, her decision to live so far away from home, were a source of heartbreak for Annie.

"She'll be home one of these days," Karl said, trying to reassure his wife.

"Perhaps for a visit," Annie said, "but she'll never come back to stay. She's like Roger. Remember Karl. The 'after you've seen Paree' syndrome."

"How could I not remember," Karl said with a wry smile. "I'm still waiting for the replacement he was going to send."

41

The winter was long and cold as week after week the temperature hovered near the zero mark. For Karl and Annie, it was more than the cold weather that discouraged them. Keeping their spirits up wasn't easy as time passed with nothing but silence from Roger Carstairs.

Spring brought endless days of rain.

"I think we're on the verge of our usual spring flu epidemic," Karl told his wife at dinner one evening.

"Oh no," Annie groaned and for the hundredth time, "When are you going to get help?" she asked.

But the flu epidemic turned out to be a false alarm with only a few scattered cases and Karl, sitting at his desk relaxing between patients, answered the phone, which no longer rang, but buzzed.

"A call from Syracuse," Connie told him.

"The fates have finally taken pity on us," Karl told his wife as he almost scared her to death, with his sudden appearance in the middle of the day.

"Roger called," he told her, hardly able to contain his enthusiasm. "He has a young doctor who wants to practice in a rural community, a community that is growing, that has a rich historical background, that is comparatively well to do. He obviously anticipates on being paid on time, and whereas starting out with an older doctor suits him fine, he wants to be able to buy the practice when the older doctor retires."

Karl finished, watching for his wife's smile of pleasure.

"I see," was all she said, momentarily too dazed by the non-stop recitation, to share in her husband's excitement.

Finally, after absorbing some of what Karl had told her, she asked, "When is this ambitious, young doctor with his and your future all planned out coming?" There was more skepticism than pleasure in her voice.

"I told Roger to send him on his way." Karl answered, undaunted by her cool reception of his news.

"For an interview, I presume," she said primly.

"I think I gave Roger the impression I'd welcome him with open arms," Karl told her, her attitude and questions starting to irritate him.

"But you haven't met him, Karl, or talked to him. How do you know he's right for Farmington? How do you know you'll like him?" Annie continued in the same critical tone.

"Annie, please," Karl begged, "stop putting obstacles in the way. If Roger thinks he's okay for Farmington, then I think he's okay for Farmington and whether I like him or not, I have no intention of letting him get away. I probably made him sound more aggressive than he is," he added, intent on calming her anxiety.

Annie, well aware of how badly her husband needed another doctor, silenced any further misgivings she might have and let the full import of Karl's news sink in. A long-promised vacation would no longer be a dream.

"I'm half way to London," she told him and saw the relief on his face.

"Things will work out, Annie," he promised. "No reason why they shouldn't. And now I have to get back to the office."

Annie walked him to the door and watched as he strode down the path to his car. "I shouldn't have been so critical of a man I haven't even met," Annie reproached herself. "Karl's step is a little lighter already."

42

Doctor Jeremy Stanley Rienhart arrived in Farmington a week after Roger's call. The office girls, Connie and Marianne had hurried to blow the stuffiness out of the office that had sat empty for so long, and now, their curiosity at its peak, awaited his arrival.

Doctor Rienhart came, not with the eager, jaunty step of his two predecessors. He did carry a black bag but he was far too professional to appear carrying wrapped documents.

The girls examined him closely.

He was reasonably tall, five-eleven or so, and trim as an athlete. His baby blue eyes and blond hair sent shivers through Marianne. Connie saw the hard line of his lips and felt his aloofness when Karl introduced him. But she had worked for Dr. Vokil too long to be disturbed by what she considered professional aloofness.

"What's the doctor like?" Annie asked her husband after their first day together. Do you like him? How soon will he be ready to take over? When can I start making plans?"

Karl laughed at the barrage of questions and told her, "We can't plan on a vacation for at least a month. I invited him for dinner on Sunday so you'll have a chance to make up your own mind as to what he's like."

But in spite of her original skepticism about the new doctor, Annie's mind was on planning their vacation.

"The first thing I have to do is go on a diet," Annie told her husband as they were getting ready for bed that night.

"Losing weight always makes you grumpy, and I never get a decent meal," Karl complained. "Besides, you look fine."

"You'd say that no matter how fat I was."

"You'll never be fat, Annie. We both know that."

"How can you say that? Do you know how many pounds I've gained lately?"

"Annie, please come to bed and worry about your weight tomorrow," Karl pleaded.

As Annie climbed into bed, she told her husband, "I just want you to be proud of me," but he was already asleep.

Emma called to share the good news. "I'm making a stop at the office to inspect the new doctor," she told her mother. "I'll stop by and we can plan on a going away party.

"No rich food," Annie told ger daughter. "I'm on a diet."

Annie was not capable of concentrating on anything that didn't relate to their trip, so when her husband mentioned that Emma had been at the office to inspect the new doctor and had mentioned a going away party, Annie had to admit she'd forgotten all about it. "I have a million things to do. Karl, would you mind if I just invite them for dinner some night before we go and skip the going away party?"

"It's up to you," he told her," then asked, "Annie are we flying or sailing?"

"I always dreamed of sailing on the Queen Mary, sitting at the captain's table for dinner, walking along the deck after dark and looking up at the stars, dancing the night away. Sailing always seemed so romantic, but when you think about it, it's an awful waste of time staring at the ocean for four days when we could be seeing Europe, don't you think?" Annie asked, looking at her husband for approval.

"Europe," Karl exclaimed. "Who said anything about Europe. I thought we were going to London."

"Well as long as we're over there, it would be a shame not to go to Paris, don't you think?" Annie said.

Karl couldn't help being moved by the pleading voice. "We'll go anywhere you want, Annie. London, Paris, Rome, Constantinople…" Annie threw her arms around her husband.

"Oh, Karl, we'll have a wonderful time. It's been so long since we've had a real vacation," she told him, her eyes sparkling with love and excitement.

"Will you make the arrangements, get the tickets, find out if we need shots, a passport, or would you rather I did it?" Karl asked Annie, knowing what her answer would be.

"Don't worry about a thing," she told him. "I've been waiting a long time for this. I want to enjoy everything from asking a million questions at every travel agency around, to getting brochures and learning as much as I can about every country we'll be visiting. I'm so excited, I probably won't sleep for the next four weeks."

"Just so you don't keep me awake," Karl told her.

True to her word, Annie had the tickets and enough information to take them around the world, twice. She even remembered to ask Dr. Rienhart to give Karl his shots. The dining room table was covered with maps and brochures. The empty bags and boxes told Karl that Annie had forgotten her diet and had been shopping. Her enthusiasm was contagious. He was getting as anxious as Annie to be on their way.

"I didn't want to start packing too soon," Annie told Karl as they sat at the kitchen table eating dinner. "I thought it would make time drag. But I've started laying a few things out on the bed in the spare bedroom. "Oh, Karl, it's so exciting."

"Jeremy is making it easy for us to leave," Karl told Annie. He already knows as much about running the office as I do and is getting to know the patients. I have a feeling it wouldn't bother him if we left tomorrow."

Annie gave her husband a long look, then told him. "I think

you should remind Jeremy that we are only going on a vacation, that you're not retiring."

Karl laughed at her. "Annie, he's only trying to have things run smoothly while we're away."

"Yes, I know," she agreed, not wanting to upset her husband with her misgivings about Jeremy Rinehart.

Annie stood by the door of their spare bedroom looking at the clothes laid out on the bed, her and Karl's, ready to be folded and packed. Each of her outfits were there, along with all the accessories, even jewelry. She splurged on new lingerie, and lacey, frilly nightgowns, plus a couple of new purses, large enough to hold brochures and maps.

There were suits and shirts for Karl. He'd pick out his ties.

Only three more days and they were off to London, Annie told herself as she stood looking at the bed and their clothes all laid out so carefully. She wasn't leaving anything to chance.

Today, Emma is coming to get the suitcases down from the attic.

"We'll get the suitcases down, go over your list, in case there are any last-minute items to shop for, then to the grill for lunch. I'll be there as close to noon as I can make it," she promised.

"Tomorrow with the suitcases down from the attic, I'll get most of the packing done. On the day before we leave, I'll go to the hairdressers and finish any last-minute packing. Emma and Will are coming to dinner. The evening will fly by." And then... Annie looked at the clock, "Another hour before Emma gets here. I think I'll make a quick trip to the attic and examine the suitcases. They've been up there for so many years, we might need a couple of new ones."

Annie climbed the steep steps to the attic and reached for the light cord. The light shone on the white sheets that covered the suitcases and when she pulled them off, she was delighted to see how clean the suitcases looked.

"I might as well take a couple of the smaller ones down to the bedroom," Annie decided and in no time, she had them all downstairs, neatly lined up at the end of the bed.

"That will save Emma doing it when she comes. One less thing to worry about," Annie told herself as she looked at the clock and realized she'd have to hurry to be ready when Emma came.

The first pain surprised Annie but didn't alarm her. "I shouldn't have been going up and down those attic stairs. I should have waited for Emma."

Annie cried out as a second pain ripped through her chest.

"I won't panic," she told herself as she held tight to the bedpost waiting for the pain to ease. "I'll go downstairs and sit in my rocker and rest until it passes."

Annie waited for the pain to ease up a little more and then gingerly holding on to the banister, Annie went down, one slow step at a time. As she passed the dining room table, she grabbed a few brochures. "If I keep my mind off the pain, it'll go away," she said aloud to calm herself.

Annie lowered herself into the rocker. The brochures fell from her hand as she grabbed her chest and called her husband's name.

43

Emma could smell the coffee the minute she walked in the house. "I'm here Mom," she hollered as she headed for the kitchen to unplug the coffee pot. When there was no answer, Emma went to the bottom of the stairs and called up, "Mom, I'm here."

It was the unusual quiet that alerted her. There wasn't a sound to be heard, not so much as a footstep. Annie had the strange feeling of being alone in the house.

"Mom," she called as she moved toward the dining room. Brochures strewn across the floor caught Emma's eye and she knew something was terribly wrong.

In spite of the fear that raced through her body at the sight of her mother's limp body, Emma did all the right things. She called an ambulance, then her father. She followed the ambulance to the hospital. "I'll call Will as soon as I get there. He'll know what to do for Dad."

Sure that her mother was dead, Emma realized how terrible this was going to be for her father. She held tight to the steering wheel trying to control the shaking of her body.

"Oh God, Dad… he'll be out of his mind… all the wonderful plans… they waited so long… don't think now or you'll end up in a ditch," Emma warned herself. "Keep your eyes and mind on the road."

It was Will who took Karl home from the hospital. "Come home with me," Will suggested, but at the very suggestion Karl threatened to get out of the car. They had reached the house when he was out of the car. He rushed up the steps, threw open the door, and began to attack everything in his path. With one swoop, the brochures went flying off the dining room table. With another swoop, the large crystal bowl and the candles were tossed violently on the dining room floor, glass flying in all directions.

There was no stopping him as he climbed the stairs and the suitcases came tumbling down, one on top of the other, empty reminders of what was to have been. With every act of violence there was a cry of pain, and anguish and outrage, and Emma knew her father was striking out at more than his wife's death as in his anger he railed against every wound he'd ever suffered, every love one he'd lost, against the futility of love when the end was pain and loneliness. He railed against a God who demanded mercy and justice from his subjects and rewarded them with the one thing which they had no recourse, death.

Emma made a move to reach out to her father but Will held her back afraid that in his unrestrained violence, he might strike out at her.

Eventually Karl's anger was spent and exhausted, he collapsed in a chair.

Will called Dr. Rinehart, who eying the broken glass gave Karl a shot and medication that would help him through the days ahead. Will helped him upstairs, undressed him and put him to bed, then went down to hold his wife as she wept in his shoulder.

Emma dreaded the days ahead, but like a man in a trance, her father survived the ritual of the funeral. Buried deep in his own sadness, he accepted condolences and kind words with a nod, occasionally a handshake. At home he moved with no discernable objective. He was in and out, from kitchen to bench where he sat for long periods, then back into the house where he nibbled on food offered to him.

Alex and Bonnie hurried home, as did Lucy. Joey was left in London with friends.

There was little time for Emma and Lucy to patch up old wounds and renew friendships.

"I'll come for a visit when I have more time," she promised Emma and asked Will to drive her to the airport the day after the funeral.

Alex delayed his return to London, intent on helping his father deal with the lonely days ahead. He spent long hours with him, walking with him, siting beside him on the bench, encouraging him to eat. Alex's quiet presence seemed to bring his father comfort.

One day he asked Alex about his work and listened while he explained the Marshall Plan and its objective, not only to rebuild but to heal the wounds of the war. He told him of his small part in the rebuilding work.

"Architect," his father said with a smile. "It rolls off my tongue quite well, don't you think, Alex?" There was no sarcasm now.

During the hours spent with his father, Alex had time to learn and think about himself as well as his father. He realized how harshly he had judged him; how intolerant he had been of his father's narrow scope of the world that seemed not to exist beyond Farmington. He hadn't given a lot of thought to what his farther had done for the people of Farmington and the surrounding territory, alone.

"I was so anxious to explain my humanitarian plans, so determined to make him and Bonnie too, see the future of the world as I saw it." Alex was ashamed now of the patronizing attitude. "Youth is so opinionated and selfish," he realized.

As they sat together on the bench, Alex encouraged his father to talk about his life on the farm and listened to the stories he'd heard as a child, sitting with his dad on this same bench.

"I completely missed the depth of Dad's feeling for his grandfather and for the farm," Alex told Bonnie as they sat alone one evening. "There's an entire part of his life that ended in tragedy, when he lost everything he loved, including a brother. But he never shared that sadness with us. We loved his stories, but they were always about the man who was determined to own a piece of land all his own, the stories were about more than just a man. Dad was telling us about a life we'd never know unless he told us. He wanted us to know about our heritage."

"Did he mention Linus?" Bonnie asked.

"No, he didn't, Bonnie," Alex said, "and I doubt he ever will. He'll sit out on the bench with his memories of mom and Linus and the part of his life that is over. We'll accuse him of spending too much time out there alone, but that's how he handles not just tragedy, but his memories." Alex didn't try to hide the sadness when he added, "Linus understood about Dad and the bench."

Bonnie felt a heavy load was taken off her shoulders as a deeper understanding developed between father and son, and told her husband, "I'd like to think that someday our children will sit with your dad on his bench and hear those same stories and learn about their heritage."

By the time Bonnie and Alex were ready to return to London, Karl was talking about going back to the office, part time for a while. They worried about him living alone.

"We'll come by as often as we can," Emma assured them. "And he enjoys the boys in small doses," she added.

"Come visit us in London," Alex invited Will and Emma. "Give Joey a chance to get to know his cousins, and a little history, first hand. Come see us now, when parts of the city are still in ruins and then come again in a few years when restoration work is near completion, and bring Dad," Alex suggested.

Alex did not tell them that he invited his father to go back with him.

"Not for a while, Alex. Not until I can make the trip without it being a memorial," he had told his son, and Alex, encouraging him to go back to the office, knew that in time, his father would come because of Joey.

As the weeks passed, Emma noticed that returning to the office hadn't dispelled her father's depression, and she attributed it to loneliness now that Alex and Bonnie had left and he was alone in the house. She came one evening with his favorite strawberry pie, hoping to cheer him up but he only nibbled on the piece Emma gave him.

"It's more than loneliness that's bothering him. He hasn't even asked about the boys, complaining because I didn't bring them, the way he usually does."

Putting out a feeler, Emma asked him, "How are things going at the office, Dad?"

When he said in a flat, hard voice, "I am not comfortable with Jeremy Rinehart," the answer was so unexpected, Emma could only stare, open mouthed.

"He's angry, she realized, and searching for something to say, she asked him, "The age difference?" aware that it could make a difference.

"To a degree, I suppose," he admitted. "The new and the old aren't mixing too well. But it's more than that, Emma. Would you be surprised if I told you, I don't like the man?"

Emma couldn't help but smile. Her father was never one to mince words, but this was serious. "Tell me about him," she suggested, sure there was more to this than her father's dislike of the man.

"I remember the day Roger called me about Jeremy. Your mother was concerned that I hadn't even met him, talked to him before telling Roger to send him as soon as possible. But, in my excitement, my need for an associate, and the weariness that had become so much a part of me, I might not have noticed our differences," he admitted.

"The tried and true methods of my generation are primitive

to him. Fresh out of school, interning in a hospital that has had time to move into the modern postwar era where new is better, I think he probably feels obliged to rescue the citizens of Farmington by introducing them to the modern world as quickly as possible. Deliberate or otherwise, I find his tolerance of me and my ways insulting," Karl said, his anger rising with each complaint.

Appalled, hardly able to believe what she was hearing, Emma was at a loss as to how to help her father. This kind of professional arrogance was something only he could deal with.

"Once he gets back to the office," was their constant refrain when the family discussed their fears about the lonely days ahead for him, but the office was piling grief upon grief.

"Have you talked, given Dr. Rienhart an indication of your plans?" Emma asked, struggling to say something that might lead to an amicable solution.

"What plans?" he asked, anger flaring. "There were no plans except to make things easy for Jeremy, to acquaint him with the community, the community he was so anxious to serve." There was disappointment as well as anger in Karl's voice as he continued. "I wonder if he isn't more ambitious than caring," he said sadly, and Emma who had worked for her father and not only seen but experienced his caring ways, could hardly believe what her father was telling her.

"He's instructed the girls not to ask the patients which doctor they want to see, and to remind them that Dr. Vokil is only in the office part time."

"But didn't he realize you'd be back full time? When you talked vacation, was there any talk of part time on your return?" Emma asked.

"There was no reason for such a discussion. We were busy getting organized so things would run smoothly while I was away. I'm sure part time never entered his mind until..."

Karl didn't finish the sentence. He was remembering Annie's

words, "Tell Jeremy you're only going on vacation, not retiring. She had misgivings about him from the beginning, but I wouldn't listen to her."

"He has moved quickly, hasn't he?" Emma said, interrupting her father's thoughts, "taking advantage of circumstances so he has a reason for what he's doing. He seems terribly anxious to take over Farmington alone."

"He hasn't been entirely honest with me," Karl said, "but I take responsibility for not asking more questions."

"I wondered about his wife, or if he had one. He does indeed have a wife. She's interning in Children's Hospital in Pittsburgh as a pediatrician, and plans to join her husband here in Farmington," Karl concluded with a deep sigh.

Emma sat staring at her father, almost as angry as he was, then asked him... "Am I right to conclude that Connie is keeping you up-to-date on what's going on in the office?"

"Connie has been working for me too long not to let me know when someone is stealing my practice," Karl told her defensively, though Emma wasn't sure if he was defending himself or Connie.

"It will be several months before his wife finishes her training, so I have a few months reprieve," he said, his words heavy with sarcasm.

"Dad, there has to be a way out of this mess. You don't have to work with a man you don't like and who is underhanded and dishonest," Emma said and reminded him, "It's your practice, you know."

"I should have listened to your mother," he said sadly, and when he told Emma, "I'll see how things go in the next few weeks," she sensed he had enough talk of Jeremy for now. His thoughts returned to Annie.

"I'll talk to Will," Emma told her father as she prepared to leave, reminding him about the pie she's put in the refrigerator.

Emma drove home struggling to understand Jeremy Rienhart.

"Is he a new breed of man, a product of the post war era, as everything seems to labelled today? He's so deliberate in his methods, making plans, working things out for the day when his wife will join him. With my mother dying and Marianne a willing conspirator, it's been so easy for him. He doesn't seem to have a qualm about what he's doing to Dad. The people of Farmington will soon find out that he's not the kind, caring doctor, they're used to."

By the time Emma arrived home she had a splitting headache but no understanding of the likes of Jeremy Rienhart.

When she explained the situation to her husband, he couldn't see why there was a problem.

"Your father can tell him to move out, set up his own practice in another location," Will said, making the entire problem seem so simple.

"You make it sound so simple, Will," Emma told him, but I don't think Dad's up to that kind of hassle. What he needs is exactly what he thought he was getting. An associate to share the responsibilities. And it would have helped Dad cope with his loss of mom… Emma's voice trailed off, tears rolling down her cheeks.

Will put his arm around her. "We'll talk to your father, Emma. We'll work it out," he promised.

Emma was right. Her father was not up to the kind of battle that would surely ensue if he tried to get Jeremy out. When Will talked to him, he shook his head and repeated what he's said all along. "I wanted and need another doctor to work with me. It's been too much for one person for a long time. There's no reason for Jeremy to be so anxious to push me out. There's work enough for both of us, at least until his wife comes and takes over the babies and children."

"Do you know how long it will be before his wife will be joining him?" Will asked.

"Jeremy said a few months. I wouldn't be surprised if she walked in tomorrow," Karl told them. "Maybe that's what the rush to get me out is all about."

But Dr. Rienhart had been truthful about his wife. There was no sign of her and in spite of Will's attempt to persuade Karl to ask Jeremy to move, he chose to continue to go to the office as usual.

There were patients who refused to see Jeremy so long as Karl was there, but the younger folks like him. Karl knew youth had its magnetism, and the new doctor was young and good looking. With Marianne in the office drooling over him, anxious to so his bidding, Jeremy's intent was evident as Karl watched her lead the patients past his office to Jeremy's.

As the days drag with fewer patients, Karl felt a little like he did when his mother sold the farm, angry and betrayed.

44

One morning as he stood shaving, Karl examined his face in the mirror. "I've aged, these past few months, Annie. And my hand isn't as steady as it should be, scraping at his heavy beard."

Talking to Annie, telling her his troubles had become a habit now that he was alone. Karl found solace in telling her about his day, and his troubles with Jeremy, though it might disturb his family if they knew. Karl grinned. "They wouldn't understand any more than they did the bench."

Suddenly, the idea of going to the office depressed him. "The joy is gone," he said aloud. "With Gary and Roger, we were a team, working together. With Jeremy, there is no teamwork. Jeremy's concern is Jeremy. I've had enough, Karl told himself with a firmness of purpose that surprised him. I'll go to the office to pick up my belongings, say goodbye to Connie and Marianne, though my leaving won't bother Marianne. Connie says she's sure stuck on Jeremy. How naïve. When Annie and I were stuck on each other, at least we were single. Karl was smiling as he remembered the day he had sat at Annie's desk and shared her brown bag lunch. Annie, Annie. I can still see your impish grey eyes and hear you laugh… ouch!" Karl let out a holler as blood spurted from his chin. Hastily he grabbed a towel and stemmed the flow. Not much more than a nick, he told himself after examining it.

Karl dressed and went down to fix his breakfast. It was a frugal meal of fruit and dry toast along with a cup of tea. Without Annie to fix his meals and sit down with him, he found eating more if a nuisance than a pleasure.

Still firm in his decision to end his association with Jeremy, Karl went down cellar in search of a box to hold the few belongings he planned on bringing home, then drove to the office, unprepared for the emotional toll this decision would have on him. Karl unlocked and went in the side door.

The smells were familiar, the quiet was not. It would be at least an hour before Connie or Marianne would be in. He had time to clear out his desk and take his certificate off the wall. He'd ask Will to bring his books. Karl sat at the desk he'd inherited from Gary, old heavy oak, with keys for every drawer, and carved fancy scrolls along each side.

I'll tell Will to take a look at it when he comes for my books. We should keep it on the family, a reminder of Gary and our happy days together.

From his leather chair that swiveled in every direction, Karl could look out the large window where the trees, in full leaf, protected the office from the hot summer sun.

Karl remembered when he first realized the buggy had truly become extinct, when only the automobile lined the street. For a fleeting moment, before he turned his eyes away, the red convertible was there, parked under the huge oak tree. Quickly, Karl shook the mist from his eyes and went to the storage closet in search of a ladder. He carried it to the office and one by one, he carefully removed the framed certificates from the wall, each one leaving its mark, the empty spaces vivid reminders of long ago when Annie had helped hang them. Hadn't she been flirting just a little that day?" Karl smiled wistfully at the recollection.

"How do you say goodbye to a lifetime of memories?" Karl asked himself as he let his eyes roam around the office. The stack of journals, some dating back to his first year in practice, were stacked neatly on one of the shelves, a reminder of the days when he'd visit Marge. And next to them were his old textbooks, every one of them, reminders of his college years, of Aaron and Julia.

Suddenly Karl had had enough of remembering and began clearing the top of his desk, putting the pictures of Annie and the children in the small cardboard box he's brought from home. Holding back tears, Connie stood at the door of the office, taking in the significance of Karl's presence, the empty wall, the small box. Karl got up and went over, and put his arm around her.

"I had thought to be out of here before anyone came." Handing Connie a clean handkerchief, he told her, "We've been friends for a long time, Connie. We've a lot of good memories. Wipe your tears and promise to come visit me once in a while. We'll have a lot to talk about."

Hurriedly, Karl began to clean out his desk drawers, discarding papers without even looking at them.

"I'll ask Will to take down the shingle that hangs outside. It's weather beaten from years of hanging there, but you can still read our names, Dr. Gary Hallan, M.D., Dr. Karl Vokil, M.D. Gary and I were so proud of that shingle. It was the beginning of a memorable partnership."

"In a few days, Jeremy Stanley Rienhart will take over my office. It's bigger than his and has a window that looks out on beautiful trees. He'll hang his diploma on the wall where mine has hung all these years. Because he belongs to this generation that is gadget happy, he'll take the intercom for granted, never knowing the fun I had buzzing Connie and Marianne, making excuses for calling them. They knew all along I was acting like a kid with a new toy."

"I'll ask Connie to carry my box out to the car. That way I can shoo her out and have a few minutes to walk through each room one last time."

Suddenly, Karl did not want to walk through the rooms one last time. Anger was again surfacing, as so often happened lately. Retirement, when it came, should be filled with a feeling of accomplishment and anticipation of days of pleasure and relaxation, not the need to fight against bitterness, and days of loneliness.

Grabbing his coat and without once turning for a backward look, he left the building, the small box of cherished possessions under his arm.

Karl resisted the urge to slam the door, but kicked a stone clear across the parking lot. The small reflex helped calm him.

Karl put the box in the car and went around to the front of the building, to stand looking up at the wooden sign, the last time he'd see it hanging there.

Epilogue

Karl's family accused him of becoming a recluse. When they found him sitting out on the bench, they accused him of dwelling on the past.

"Of course, I dwell on the past," he wanted to tell them. "What else is there but the past to fill my thoughts when the future no longer holds promise."

Will came one evening with the boys, Michael and Hughie. The boys went looking for their Grandpa and found him sitting outside on the bench.

"Grandpa, Grandpa," they hollered in unison as they ran toward him. "Can I sit on the bench with you, Grandpa?" Michael asked. "Me too," Hughie echoed.

With one hand Karl reached down too lift Hughie on the bench while with the other he steadied Michael.

"Will you tell us a story, Grandpa?" Michael asked. "Ya," Grandpa, tell us a story," Hughie repeated.

Karl looked down from one grandson to the other. Warmed by their affection, he began to tell them a story.

"I'll bet you've never been for a ride in a buggy pulled by a horse, have you?" he asked them.

"A real horse?" they replied in unison.

"Yes, a real horse," he told them.

"I remember the first time I took your grandmother for a ride in the buggy." The voice grew soft, nostalgic, as the eyes gazed off somewhere beyond their vision. "It was a beautiful spring day, when the sun was shining and a gentle breeze blowing in her hair..."

Standing by the back door, Will smiled, as he watched his son's siting next to their Grandpa on his old wooden bench, faces upturned, listening to the story of his ride in a horse drawn buggy, and the beautiful, young girl by his side.

Printed in the United States
By Bookmasters